I0728010

Felix Publishing 2022
email: info.felixpublishing@gmail.com
Print copies available from publisher.

The Ghost and Detective McNab Casebook

Print Edition
ISBN: 978-1-925662-48-1
Digital Edition
ISBN: 978-1-925662-49-8
Author: Dr Peter T. Scott

Registration:
Thorpe-Bowker +61 3 8517 8342
email: bowkerlink@thorpe.com.au

This is a work of fiction. The characters in this book did not exist and the politics of the time have been generalized. Some of the places described are real and are well-known to the author. No disrespect is meant to any person living or dead.

The Ghost
and
Detective McNab
Casebook

Peter T. Scott

First released 2022

Table of Contents

A Misplaced Body

1.

Detective Constable Hamish McNab sat on the front step of the old, steeply tiered lecture room; his head buried in his hands wondering what in heavens name he was doing there. He had, of course, been sent out by Police Headquarters here in Edinburgh to investigate a possible murder in the Old Medical School at Edinburgh University. The only problem was that there was no body; a few traces of blood and a deserted lecture room.

The students of that previous lecture, its deliverer, Associate Professor Sinclair and his Demonstrator, Dr. McAndrew, had apparently left the room as soon as the lecture had concluded. "It bein' the lecture afore lunch, sir," the porter, who was standing apprehensively with his cap in his hand, said. He had found the body slumped over in the second-last row of the seats when he had gone in to set the room up for the afternoon lecture during the lunch break. Seeing the body and its blood, he had panicked and immediately rushed out to call the police but when he returned, the body had gone.

McNab did not feel at all happy with the situation nor with himself. He felt totally useless and unsure of himself. This was not a common emotion for the young detective on his first case; it was only that the station was short-staffed that they had not sent anyone more senior than a Probationary Detective Constable. It was not too long ago when he was a confident uniformed policeman on the cobbled streets of the old town. He had just finished a part-time degree in Science as well as his necessary studies within the Detective Branch and now was looking forward to a bright career. His promotion had soon come and he had been made up to Probationary Detective Constable but he had found that life as a plain-clothed detective was not all that he had imagined. The fact that he had gained a First-Class Honours degree did not help with his relationship with the 'Old Guard' at Headquarters who regarded him as being 'too smart for his own good'. The fact that his uncle, Sir Henry McNab was on the board of Police Commissioners also did not help.

His first few months as a junior detective had been an awkward period of his life and he had soon got over the friendly gibes of his new colleagues about his name, 'McNab' "Wha are ye gaun'ae nab today, Hamish?" usually came from Detective Sergeant McGregor on a bad day. Life in Auld Reekie, as some called the beautiful and ancient city of Edinburgh, often could be professionally unsettling. Some of his colleagues, all of whom were his superiors, considered his promotion as an intrusion.

He felt that he had been assigned to this case in the hope that he would fail and then be sent back to Uniform Branch in disgrace. Detective Hamish McNab sat on the front step in the old lecture room with his head in his hands wondering what he would do next.

"Where had the body gone?" he said to himself in a state of near panic.

Suddenly a voice, close at hand, replied: "Where else would you put a body in a medical school? Why! The Cadaver Room, of course!"

McNab looked up and around the old lecture room. It was still deserted, the dust and gloom were its only occupants. He jumped up in a state of shock. Where had that voice come from? He looked around again; he rushed up the central aisle, looking along the rows of the many seats in each tier and then he rushed down to the front of the room to look behind the long bench at the front from where the lecturer had delivered the lesson. Nothing! Nobody!

Suddenly the voice came again, just as close as before: "Oh all right! I guess that I should introduce myself".

A faint blue mist seemed to suddenly appear out of the air right in front of McNab who just gaped at the apparition. It eventually resolved itself into the figure of a man dressed in the sombre attire of a nineteenth-century gentleman; high collar, cravat, waistcoat and long frock coat. The figure went through a short period of transparency and then finally became totally visible; just like any other man except that his attire was of a bygone age. His face was not unpleasant, and a full head of hair which had once been dark but was now uniformly white, a high forehead, a high-nosed acute face with a pair of penetrating grey eyes. He smiled and said:

"Permit me to name myself as Doctor Joseph Bell, and this was once my lecture hall. Please do not alarm yourself, young man! As you can see, I have not been here, in body at least, for some time. In fact, I departed this Earth on October the fourth, in the year of our Lord nineteen hundred and eleven."

McNab sat down suddenly on the step in the first row and shook his head. He didn't believe in ghosts and although he had been told by some of his more ungracious colleagues back at Headquarters that The Old Medical School was probably haunted, he had only laughed at the suggestion. Afterall, he had an Honours Degree in Science and ghosts were not proven by the Scientific Method. The apparition, now seemingly as solid as the next man, sat down on the seat next to McNab.

"You may have heard of me perhaps?" he said, a look of expectation in his deep penetrating eyes. "As I said before, I was once a lecturer here in the Medical School, although it was not quite up to the antiquity of being called the 'Old medical School'. It was my old Alma Mater as well, if you want to use the word, old" He sighed and looked around at the old room with its faded charts, wooden seats, benches really, raised up from the main floor in a series of closely-spaced tiers. "One of my better students was a chap by the name of Arthur Conan Doyle. Perhaps you have heard of him?"

McNab had heard of him vaguely. "Wasn't he a writer of some sort?" he said in all innocence. Unfortunately, so far in his young life, literature other than scientific textbooks and Standard Operating Procedures for Police Officers had not been on his reading list.

The ghostly Bell went a little bit more transparent so that McNab could see the opposite wall through his body. It was something which he did uncontrollably when he was excited. He looked down at the young man with semi-transparent and sad eyes.

"Och! You haven't been out much have you? Yes, Doyle was one of my better students in this very room. Now, when was that? Ah yes! I believe it was in the winter of 1876 that he first enrolled. He seemed to be a very confident young man; not to dissimilar to you, my young detective, eh?"

McNab looked up at the spirit who had now regained his opaqueness and gave a weak smile. The spirit stood up and paced back and forth across the lecture room's floor and continued:

"Well then! To continue with my brief introduction. Doyle was a good student. He was my clerk for a while at the Infirmary – another one of my haunts." He laughed softly. "He was probably a satisfactory physician – he came from a poor background, you know, but luckily had a rich uncle." The spirit said, touching the side of his nose with his forefinger.

"Yes, I know what that's like!" replied McNab looking down at his dirty boots with a sigh.

"So, the young student Doyle took to writing in the hope that he should gain some wealth. But like most authors, found that publishers were generally not interested unless you were already famous – which he wasn't. Eventually, he did achieve success when he started writing his now famous stores about that eccentric detective with the deer-stalker cap and outrageous pipe. Ridiculous, I thought! Especially when some of the Penny Dreadful press suggested that Doyle had based his pompous protagonist on me! What an affront!"

The spirit went very transparent again. Almost to the point of disappearing completely, but eventually he calmed down and returned to a more solid form.

"Well, never mind!" he eventually said, sitting down on the chair next to McNab.

"We ghosts, as you call us, have great sensitivity and can still feel many of the emotions of the living such as yourself. We don't usually come down from 'upstairs' as I may euphemistically call where we come from; 'heaven' is what some call it, or 'paradise' and so on. But really it is not 'up' anywhere. The concept of people in white robes sitting on clouds playing harps is totally ridiculous! We simply call it 'home' and it is a …well, simply a different dimension to yours, if you like; and a very personal one at that. We tend to keep to our own personal family sub-dimension, but we can move about if we choose. Some spirits – I prefer that term to 'ghost', by the way – do rarely come into your dimension either out of revenge, nostalgia or simply because they are extremely confused with their sudden death and are reluctant to come to Home to be with their previously departed relatives or friends. Mostly, my fellow spirits simply wish to keep to themselves. Public hauntings are left to the deranged minds of members of the living for one reason or another. In my case, I just have a nostalgic feeling in revisiting my old 'happy places'; here in the Old Medical School and in the old buildings of the Edinburgh Infirmary."

The spirit gave a deep sigh and suddenly jumped up. "Well, more than enough about me and my life….er should that be death, young man? Oh! and before you ask me to go back Home and ask the spirit of this poor man who killed him, that would be rather difficult. His spirit, probably in a state of shock by now, would be in his own personal dimension. It would be like me asking you to go out into your wide world and find a stranger from a photograph. Near impossible! By the way, I haven't had the pleasure of a formal introduction?" He said, leaning down and looking closely into the seated McNab's face.

The young detective stood up and offered his hand then awkwardly withdrew it: "Umm…McNab, Hamish McNab." He stammered.

"Well, that's at least a good Scottish name, not like that southern invention of Doyle's unbelievable detective. But come, we have a body to find!"

2.

Having resolved to head to the Cadaver Room and look for the missing body, the spirit moved quickly up the tiered aisle towards the open rear double doors of the lecture room. McNab was astounded that the spirit had flown through the air rather than made actual steps and so he had to run up the steps quickly, taking several at each stride.

Outside, the spirit continued to effortlessly glide past the lift and down the wide staircase with its ornate wooden banisters. McNab followed as quickly as he could. Down they went, past the ground floor offices and into the basement. At the foot of the stairs, McNab looked to his left and then to his right. Further down the darkened corridor he saw the spirit leaning against the wall opposite a set of double doors, each of which had small circular windows cut into them at about head height.

"The Cadaver Room," said the spirit pointing a long white hand towards the doors. "This is where the Medical School keeps its freshly donated bodies for later use, or perhaps I should say 'abuse' by careless medical students who have yet to learn which end of a scalpel has the sharp blade attached."

McNab quickly walked up to the doors and tried the latch. Locked! He stood back and looked forlornly at the spirit who made a sound of exasperation and simply disappeared right through the door. There was a sharp clicking sound and the latch suddenly moved; unlocked from inside. The left-hand door swung open; its interior latch held by the spirit who swept his hand across his body:

"Pray enter, Detective McNab. There are some advantages in being dead as you have just witnessed. Now, let us look for the missing body."

The Cadaver Room was long, distinctly cold and lit by only one single globe in the centre of its high, arched roof. Along one side was a series of cabinets, stacked upon each other in threes and each with hinged metal doors. These doors were similar to that of the small ice-chest which McNab had remembered from his grandmother's kitchen in her old stone house in Stockbridge. These were the refrigerated lockers in which the bodies were kept.

"At lot better arrangement than the poor ice cabinets in my day." Remarked the spirit who was standing back across the wide room leaning on the zinc-covered bench which ran along the opposite wall almost for its entire length. "Now, there looks like about thirty cabinets here. Where would you hide a body if you were in a hurry, detective?"

McNab moved over to where the spirit was standing and looked at the long row of thirty cabinets set in threes along the opposite wall.

"Well, if I was in a hurry to stash a body, I would probably take the one nearest to the door, and probably the one at waist height if I was carrying the body or had it on a trolley."

The spirit clapped his hand over his knee, gave a short laugh and come up to McNab. "Good boy! At last, you are starting to show some deductive reasoning! Bravo!"

Grasping the handle of the centre cabinet nearest the door, he turned the latch and opened the door to its full extend. He pulled out the moveable shelf containing the body and looked down at the white object lying on the shelf and covered with a flimsy, white sheet. There was a large label tied with string on the big toe of its right foot which stuck out from under the sheet next to McNab's hand.

"Do you think that this is our body, Dr. Bell?" McNab asked, turning to the spirit.

"Och, now! Think again Hamish. Would you have time to strip and label a freshly-killed body if you were the murderer and in a great hurry to hide your victim?" There was friendly scorn on the spirit's face, his left eyebrow raised.

"No! You're right of course, Dr. Bell," and he pushed the shelf and its white occupant back into its cabinet and tried the one below it. Nothing. This cabinet and the upper one were both empty. McNab was disappointed in the failure of his hypothesis but moved across and tried the next cabinet at waist height. Success!

As he began to slide out the shelf, he instantly saw that this body must be the one which they had been seeking. It was fully dressed, uncovered by any sheet and its feet were still shod and unlabelled. McNab pulled the shelf out to its full extent and moved around to the right-hand side of the body. The spirit had quickly moved around to the opposite side.

"Look!" the spirit said. "Here is the wound!"

McNab moved around to the spirit's side of the shelf and saw that he was pointing to a small blood stain which had dried on the upper chest of the body near its upper left arm. The victim seemed to be a young man dressed in a long-sleeved white shirt, blue jeans and a brown waist coat. A pair of white and rather worn joggers over black socks covered his feet. The victim's skin had already turned a pale white and his lips were blue.

The spirit lifted up the body's left arm, bent it at the elbow and then let it drop back to the shelf. "As you can observe, my young friend, rigor mortis has not yet taken over the body. However, there are some traces of the muscles on his face beginning to stiffen. Can you see those line there on his cheek? Hardly wrinkles on such a young man."

McNab closely peered at the body's face and saw that there were indeed lines on the sides of the face which had formed where the muscles were located just below the white skin.

The spirit lifted up the right eyelid of the body. "There! You see! The cornea is beginning to cloud up and there is also some segmentation of the blood vessels as well. What do you think of that, detective?"

McNab leaned over and peered into the dead eye of the victim and noticed the changes which the spirit had pointed out. With some degree of satisfaction on his face, the spirit turned to McNab and said with some firm confidence.

"Well, as rigor mortis has yet to fully set in and judging from the victim's eye, I would say that he was killed at least one half of an hour ago and certainly not longer than two hours – probably shorter. At what time did you get the call to come to the crime?"

"Exactly at twelve minutes past one, sir." McNab, replied, somewhat in awe of Bell's diagnosis.

"Ah! Just I had thought! The lecture, if my memory is still good over all of these years and assuming that the

Old Medical School still operates on old traditions, would have promptly finished at five minutes to the hour. As I doubt that student behaviour has changed over the lifetime of this old institution, and it was the pre-lunch lecture, I assumed that there would have been the usual mad rush for the doors at its completion to get out for their scran."

McNab had always done his studies parttime and could only visualise the pre-lunch rush for the doorway. He also had never felt the need to linger in any lecture room but getting back home in the bleak late Edinburgh evenings was his main concern.

The spirit continued: "That would narrow the time of death down to probably between one in the post meridian and your twelve minutes later. This would be most consistent with my observations of the state of the body."

"But when was the body removed?" asked McNab.

The spirit looked thoughtfully about, his hand coming up to stroke his beardless chin.

"I would say that that it was done almost immediately after the Porter had rushed off to make the call, say about thirteen or fourteen minutes after one. When did the Porter return to the lecture room?"

"Well, almost immediately, I believe. He went back to close the doors so that the room would not be further disturbed and found the body missing. As Headquarters got the call at twelve past the hour and allowing for the time that he would take to return to the lecture room, say about five minutes, that would have been about seventeen to eighteen minutes after one. I arrived about one half hour after the call at twelve minutes past, that is about one forty-two."

"So!" said the spirit with some confidence "the poor man was murdered somewhere between say, one post meridian and seven minutes past the hour, assuming that the Porter would take about five minutes to get to the telephone. Then, having observed the departure of the Porter, the murderer would have removed the body between that time and when the Porter returned about five minutes later."

"That's a very short time span for a murder and disposal of the body, Dr Bell!" McNab stated.

"Exactly, my young sir. Our murderer was quick about his business. He would have done the job – no witnesses so far – and then kept out of sight of the Porter and waited until his departure before removing the body. As I noted several medical trolleys out in the corridor as we left, I assume that our fast friend would have thrown the body aboard one of them and then quickly taken it down that lift contraption to the Cadaver Room and stowed the body in this cabinet."

The spirit returned to the left-hand side of the body and gestured with his hand: "Open his shirt will you please, young fellow, so that I can inspect the wound. You should also find a bottle of alcohol in that cupboard over there, if traditions still hold here, and there is a towel is at the end of the bench."

McNab quickly opened the body's waistcoat and pulled up its white shirt, exposing the wound now covered in a mass of congealed blood. Leaving the body, he went over to the cupboard and found, as expected, the bottle of alcohol. Returning to the body, he gave it to the spirit who dashed some of the alcohol onto the small towel: "Another good spirit put to use, ay?" he laughed, and wiped the wound area clean.

"Ah! Just as I expected! Note the size of the wound, detective. Small, isn't it? Now, be a good fellow and find me a Surgical Probe. It should be back in that cupboard; it will be a long metal thing looking like a knitting needle but with a blunt end."

McNab returned to the cupboard and found a tray of metal surgical instruments lying on one of the shelves. Searching through them, he found the probe and returned to the body. The spirit took it and poked it into the wound; it went in almost to its hilt.

"Now, some more of your observations if you please, young sir!" the spirit asked, pulling the probe out of the body's wound.

McNab looked down at the body and the probe in Bell's hand.

"Well, It's a small wound. Only about a centimetre long, narrow and very deep."

"Exactly! About a quarter of an inch wide, very narrow and deep; almost the entire length of the probe. There can only be one instrument which would make such a wound and that is a Surgical Scalpel. Moreover, do you see where the wound enters the body? "

To McNab's observation, the wound was near the left of centre of the body just below the left nipple. So, he looked up at the spirit for further explanation.

"That scalpel would have entered the rib cage just to the side of the Sternum between the fifth and sixth rib and entered the heart causing instant death through shock. Moreover, the small size of the wound would only give a small amount of blood, especially if the scalpel was left in the body. The few drops of blood on the floor of the lecture room would suggest that. What does that suggest?"

McNab looked up with an enthusiastic grin: "Why, only someone trained in surgery would be able to do that so precisely."

"Capital! My boy. Capital! And also, it would have to be someone who had access to this room. Remember that I had to open its lock from the inside for us to gain access."

"Right, then!" exclaimed McNab. That would suggest the lecturer, Dr. Sinclair or his Demonstrator, both of whom could have killed their victim and then lingered behind in the Preparation Room behind the front of the lecture room until the Porter left the body and then trolleyed it downstair."

"True!" said the spirit, but such a wound could also have been inflicted by anyone in the room who had at least three years training. I think that you said that this was a special lecture given to the general public and any of the students. Any one of those who had superior surgical training and was armed with a scalpel, could have finished our victim off during the melee to get to lunch and then hidden outside in the stairwell waiting to get rid of the body. It is also not unknown for senior students to have access to the Cadaver Room. I remember that as a student here myself, we would often congregate there in the cool and quietness; copies of the key were often obtained from the Purser – at a price, you understand."

McNab looked down at the floor, disheartened. There were probably over one hundred students in the room according to the Porter and many of these would have been senior students with the knowledge of how to commit such a crime and also access to the room in the basement. Besides, a medical student wheeling a body down to the Cadaver Room would not arouse many suspicions if seen by any staff or other students.

The spirit moved over to the long bench which occupied the other side of the room opposite the cabinets. There was a small flat-box sterilizer of the old type sitting on the bench. "You notice that the murder weapon was no longer in the victim even though it had been pushed all of the way in. So! What would a murderer do with his weapon when in a hurry and not wanting it to be found? Well, now! The most likely place for a scalpel would be in such a sterilizer as this one," he said with confidence unclamping and lifting up the top of the sterilizer. "Hey presto! The murder weapon, I believe!"

McNab walked over and looked into the sterilizer which contained a single, long-handled scalpel. "Well, I'll be...!" he said.

"Alas, laddie! The sterilizer's still warm. We'll not be getting fingerprints off this scalpel," he said sadly. "There is also the problem of motive, I believe. Don't you detective fellows look for that to narrow down your list of suspects?"

"That's true enough, Dr. Bell," McNab said, getting even more discouraged.

"Out of my sphere, you understand, but let's search the victim's clothing. I'll warrant that our murderer, in his hurry, had little time to do that. As your forensic people -that's what they are called? – should be here any minute, it's unlikely that the murderer has yet returned to finish turning this poor soul into just another cadaver.

McNab took the advice given and started at the pockets in the shirt and waistcoat of the victim and then down to the pockets of the trousers. They were in luck. Apart from some loose change in a waistcoat pocket, McNab found a wallet in the victim's back pocket when he had turned the body over. He carefully took out his handkerchief and extracted the wallet from the victim's back pocket. Surprisingly, when opened, it contained a few high-denominational notes and a Royal Bank of Scotland credit card which identified the victim as one Simon Elliott; nothing else. The young detective went to put the wallet into a collection bag which he carried in his pocket when a small piece of folded paper fell out of one of the open compartments.

He bent down, picked up the paper and unfolded it. It contained a series of numbers:

831919   130784868

"What do you make of these numbers, Dr Bell?"

The spirit glanced at the paper and shook his head. "Nothing comes to me right now, so further investigation by you will be needed, I think."

Suddenly there came a distant shout, "McNab! Where are you?"

The spirit looked, at the detective and raised his left eyebrow. "Och now! It looks like your friends from the station have at last arrived. Time for my departure it would seem. But listen, laddie, yon piece of paper will need some close examination. Put that and the wallet into your little bag as evidence." He turned and walked towards the door of the room and turned momentarily. "Should you be needing my assistance again, just come to the old lecture room – preferably at night when there is nobody else in the building – and just call my name. It is one of my old haunts!" He gave a little laugh as his body became transparent and then disappeared in a trail of light blue vapour.

McNab stuffed the folded piece of paper back into the wallet and them put it into his evidence bag which he quickly stuffed into his own trousers pocket. He stood for a while gazing at the spot where his ghostly friend had disappeared. He shook his head to clear his thoughts and went to the open door of the Cadaver Room. "Down here!" he called out loudly.

He was soon joined by a thick set man of middle age with glasses and a grey bushy moustache; Detective Chief Inspector MacFarlane, chief of the local CID. With him were two men in white coats and carrying small suitcases.

"Now, McNab! What are you doing down here, eh?" said DCI MacFarlane looking over his metal-rimmed glasses. He folded his arms tightly across his broad chest and remarked: "It certainly has got cold all of a sudden. What is this room? A morgue?"

McNab waved his hand around the room and with a confident smile of an actor who had just rehearsed his lines said: "Almost sir! We were missing a body, so I came down to the very place where one could quickly and easily stash one in a hurry – the Cadaver Room of the Medical School. And I think that I have found our murder victim, one Simon Elliott, possibly a senior medical student; unless the medical school now stores cadavers fully dressed!"

"Well! Ummm…good work, young man. Anything else?"

McNab moved over to the left-hand side of the body and lifted up its shirt and waistcoat again and pointed to the wound. "You will see here, sir, that the wound is only a small, linear one and made expertly between the fifth and sixth rib. Moreover, when a probe was inserted into it, the wound was shown to be very deep and reached the heart itself; the sort of incision which suggests the skill of a medical man or at least a Third-Year medical student. It was made by using a long-handled scalpel. In addition, "McNab continued, lifting the left arm of the body up and letting it drop again, "you will notice that rigor mortis has not yet fully set in. The corneas of his eyes are beginning to cloud up and there is also some segmentation of the blood vessels. This also suggest that this must be our murder victim as he has only been dead for, say half an hour to an hour."

The DCI and the two forensic men looked at the young detective with some awe. MacFarlane closed his opened mouth and then opened it again saying: "That is a remarkable piece of deduction, detective. Well done! I don't suppose that you have also found the murder weapon, eh?" he said looking at the young man with a doubting sidelong glance.

"In the sterilizer over there, I think sir. Another obvious place to put a scalpel," he said, pointing to the old-fashioned flat metal sterilizer sitting on the long bench. McNab looked at the older of the two forensic men and added: "I doubt that you will find any finger prints on it as the box had recently be used and is still warm."

DCI MacFarlane walked over and clapped McNab on the shoulder. "That's a remarkable piece of detective work! Sound deductions all along. Almost as good as that fictional detective fellow of that novelist who was also a student here – what was his name? Yes! Conan Doyle.

3.

Back at the unattractive complex of buildings in Fettes Avenue which housed Police Scotland's Headquarters, Probationary Detective Constable sat at his little, cluttered desk in a corner of a large room filled with other small, cluttered desks. His morning had been an exciting one and his new friendship with Dr. Joseph Bell, who had been dead for over one hundred years, had been still an unsettling experience.

The ghost's detailed observations and intuitive deductions had led to their finding the missing body of the murder victim at the Old medical School at Edinburgh University as well as considerable detail about the victim's cause of death. Such details were later confirmed by the forensic team which had arrived with DCI MacFarlane and its members now had a much different view of his young, newly promoted detective.

Despite McNab's newly found kudos, as the word had spread around the station about his remarkable deductions, the young detective was still deeply puzzled. The piece of paper which had fallen out of the victim's wallet and its mysterious set of numbers was the main cause of his puzzlement. The other problem was the lack of a mobile phone which was almost a universal attachment for students at the university. This was at least one oversight by his mentor, Dr Bell who had little experience with such a modern and ubiquitous device.

As was his usual habit, he put his head down between his hands, his elbows resting on his cluttered desk and tried to think about a possible meaning for the sets of numbers on the paper. The darkness of gloom and defeat had set in again when a friendly voice interrupted his confused thoughts.

"So! Why is the 'detective-of-the-hour' looking so glum?"

McNab looked and turned around to see his new female colleague, Detective Sergeant Olivia Kerr standing behind his chair. He was startled by this visit and his heart had begun to race. DS Kerr was perhaps the most beautiful woman he had ever seen and this was the first time that she had ever seem to notice the young detective. As a young uniformed officer, he had only been able to admire her from a distance and thought that she was even more remote as a possible friend. Even now, only a few weeks later, and with a promotion to Detective Branch, he still felt that this beautiful young woman was on a much higher plane to his lowly existence. Of medium height, and well-shaped, she had pale, flawless skin, long thick blond hair which came down in curved tresses to her shoulders, and her eyes were an alert hazel colour. She was about McNab's age but already a Detective Sergeant who also had a reputation for being the most intelligent detective in the station. She also was considered well beyond the reach of most mortal men; well, that was the opinion of the younger men of the station and some of the older as well.

McNab jumped up and found that he was standing very close to this beautiful apparition. "Ummm…. Hello" was all that he could stammer. "Yes. Ummm….thank you. I do have a few things on my mind."

DS Kerr smiled and put out a slender, white hand which McNab carefully took in his. "My name is Olivia…and yours is, I believe Hamish. Am I right?"

"Errr… yes. That's right, DS Kerr…errr Olivia." He said with a stammer.

"You certainly impressed the Gaffer!" she said, referring to their superior DCI MacFarlane. "And the forensic boys were beside themselves with the amount of detail you gave them. All confirmed by their scientific examinations, of course." She gave a wicked smile. "Oh! And you were right about that scalpel, it probably was the murder weapon and no, there weren't any fingerprints on it."

McNab gave a weak smile and looked down at his feet.

"Oh! Don't be so glum, Hamish. What is worrying you? Can I help?"

"Well, I would like that. I'm not sure as to where to go next and there is this conundrum." He said this with some new confidence as he reached down and picked up the wallet and drew out the credit card and the folded piece of paper which he had taken from the victim's pocket. DS Kerr took the piece of paper and unfolded it.

"Why, this is no problem at all, Hamish. The credit card tells us the victim's name, one Simon Elliott, and the two numbers on the piece of paper are those of a bank account." She turned the paper over so that McNab could see them. "Look! The first number is a Sort Code which identifies the bank and its branch. The second set of numbers is the actual account which its owner has at that bank. Come over to my desk and we will look them up. I can access the Banking

Commission's site which will tell us exactly where this bank is located". With that, she walked smartly across to the other side of the room where she had a much larger and less cluttered desk looking out over a lush green park and over the distant rooftops of the city.

She sat down at her desk and called up the banking site on the internet then typed the six-digit code shown on the piece of paper into its search engine.

"Ah! Here we are! No problems at all. It is the Nicolson Street Branch of the Royal Bank of Scotland. Not far from your murder scene, if my knowledge of the district serves me right. The other number is the number of the account's owner. Unfortunately, I don't have the security to access this, so we will have to go down to the bank itself and see its manager."

McNab was greatly encouraged by the use of the pronoun 'we'. His social life was suddenly looking up. He muttered something about having to go back to the Medical School and interview its staff and students and knew that this was not going to help his relationship with DS Kerr.

Instead, she simply smiled again and said: "Of course. That is the most important priority in this case." She looked pensive and then continued: "I'll tell you what! I'm between cases at the moment and your detailed findings really interest me. How about I telephone this bank manager and make an appointment with him for tomorrow. They tend to be old fuddy duddies who hold to traditional methods and don't like the police suddenly showing up; it upsets the customers, they say." She gave a wicked grin. "Besides, to them I am probably just a 'pur wee lassie' - too young and blonde to know anything about banking. They will naturally treat me with some paternal condescension and answer all of my naïve questions in banking terms which I am not supposed to understand. Several years in the Fraud Squad and a degree in economics will soon give us all of the information we need to know. Then you can buy me lunch. Deal?"

McNab was flabbergasted but grateful for both this professional help and the chance to take the lovely DS Kerr out to lunch – if he could afford it. He thanked her for her suggestion and agreed that she would have a much better chance of getting information out of some pompous bank manager than a nervous, young Probationary Detective Constable.

"Good! It's settled then!" she said." So, I'll see you tomorrow and with luck, we will know all about this account number." With that, she pulled out a small, pink notebook and quickly wrote down the name and number of the credit card and the two numbers from the piece of paper then turned and walked back to her desk to make the telephone call.

McNab was feeling that the pace of this investigation was moving faster than his new promotion could handle; he had found the body of the murder victim missing; he had befriended a ghost who was an expert in deductive reasoning; and now had met a beautiful and intelligent colleague who was interested in his work. Where to next? The answer was obvious; he needed to interview the staff and students who were present at the lecture and find a motive for the crime. It was now well after noon but he thought that he could still achieve some progress by returning to the Old Medical School.

It was only a short walk to the solid stone building of the Old Medical School and he felt somehow inadequate in returning to that building of the Victorian age; the age of Arthur Conan Doyle's great fictional detective. Entering through the imposing archway, he walked across the central courtyard with its pavement of small, grey rectangular bricks and entered the open double brown doors which led to the school's reception area.

The, the middle-age secretary in her prim white blouse looked over a pair of square-cut spectacles at the young detective's proffered badge. Reluctantly, she informed him that Professor Sinclair was probably still in his office and picked up the telephone to ask the good man if he wished to see a policeman.

After a brief conversation, she put down the telephone and pointed to a flight of stairs opposite her desk in what would have been the original entrance hallway of the old building. "Up the stairway. Turn left an' third door along. His name is on it, sae ye wonae get lost!" she said in a voice that suggested that McNab's visit was just another unwanted interruption to her day.

McNab followed her directions and knocked at the door bearing the gold-engraved title 'Associate Professor Alloysius Sinclair'. There was a gruff "enter" and McNab went in.

Sinclair's study was much as McNab had expected; book lined, high ceilinged, an old brown sofa near the door and a big desk in front of two tall windows which obviously looked out over the courtyard. The man behind the desk also was as expected, being in his later years with sparse grey hair around the ears on an almost bald head, a slightly grey face, small intense brown eyes and a double chin.

As McNab entered, the professor stood up and extended a long, bony hand across the desk. "Well, now! What may the police department want at this late hour?" McNab took the cold hand which now waved down towards a chair which was at the side of the desk. "Sit! Sit, yourself down, young man and tell me what you want. I suppose it's about that dreadful event at my last lecture? I don't have much time, ye ken? It's well past my day's work in this old mausoleum." He said with just a trace of a smile on his old face.

McNab sat down, feeling somewhat like an errant schoolboy who has just been called to the Head's office for a 'taking to'. He composed his thoughts and asked the professor the usual questions about the 'dreadful event'; what did he do when he finished? Did he see anything out of the ordinary? What did he do at the end of the lecture? What did Demonstrator McAndrew do at the end of the lecture; and about the students who had left in the usual rush to get to their food.

Professor Sinclair, true to bis naturally abrupt nature and the need to rid himself quickly of the irritation of being questioned, replied in a series of brief numbered answers:

1. No! He did not see anything 'out of the ordinary' (his emphasis) as he was carefully watching and describing Dr. McAndrew's new technique in reconnecting the sciatic nerve of a leg;

2. At the end of the lecture, he went back into the preparation room behind its blackboard where Mr. Tomlinson, the Theatre Assistant had taken the dissected leg and the other items used in the dissection. He then had accompanied Mr. Tomlinson, who was taking the remains to the School's incinerator, as far as the stairwell;

3. Demonstrator Iain McAndrew had stayed behind and to the best of his knowledge, followed the students out of the lecture room via the rear doors; and

4. He had not been present when all of the students had departed but they usually did not linger, especially just before lunch.

When finished, the professor looked at McNab with some satisfaction at having the answers to all of his questions but he also added that:

"The audience was a mixed bunch of both students and the general public. It was an advertised, special demonstration on a new technique and was thus open to all. Being an extracurricular event for the students, it would also offer accrued assessment marks for attendees and so a roll was taken before the beginning of the lecture. This will be available from the secretary downstairs. Good day."

McNab took the sudden dismissal, thinking that he had received all of the answers which he needed and went back downstairs to ask for the location of Dr. McAndrew's room and for a printout of the students who had attended the fatal lecture.

The secretary informed him that Dr. McAndrew had left for the day and would not return until the next. She reluctantly searched her computer for the roll taken at the lecture which, luckily also included the personal particulars of the students such as their level of study and contact details. Satisfied with that, he went across the courtyard to the other set of doors which led up another staircase to the old lecture room where he hoped to renew his acquaintance with Dr, Bell.

Just as he hoped, the corridor and the staircase leading to the lecture room upstairs had been cordoned off with copious amounts of blue and white tape worded with 'No Entry – Police Crime Scene'; the uniformed boys had been very busy. He climbed through the tape and went upstairs and into the darkened lecture room. The afternoon lectures had been cancelled, the area was deserted and in partial darkness. McNab sat down on the aisle chair in the top tier and gently called:

"Dr. Bell. Are you there?" It occurred to him that his soft call was typical of those 'not wanting to wake the dead' and that it was exactly the opposite to what he wanted. It was rather comical when he thought about it and he stifled a quiet laugh. Eventually, there was the expected wisp of luminous blue smoke which gradually resolved itself into the opaque body of his new friend, Dr. Joseph Bell, MD.

"Well, greetings my young detective. What more have you found out about your case?" The spirit stood in the aisle just down from where McNab was sitting.

"Well, not as much as I would like, Dr. Bell. I have a list of the students who were at the lecture and have determined that Associate Professor Sinclair probably was not in the room when the murder was committed. His Demonstrator, Dr. McAndrew also apparently departed quickly with the students."

"Ah! Very interesting. Let us consider the departure of the students then," said the spirit, gliding quickly up the aisle to the rear set of double doors. "The body was sitting here in the second-last row, you said? Sitting mind, not slumped over or fallen?"

"No." McNab replied. "The Porter said that he had thought that the man had simply gone to sleep, not uncommon in such lectures. His body was sitting upright and only his head was down on his chest."

"Well, now!" said the spirit. "This would suggest that he was probably alive at the start of the exodus and was killed as the students went past him as they left. It would seem unlikely that those in the upper seats, who would have gone out first, would have done the deed as their fellows would have seen them do it. Remember that the wound was on the left-hand side of the body and the victim sat in the right-hand side of the aisle. This would mean that the murderer would have had to lean across the body to give the hard, fatal jab. The right side of the victim's body would have been more convenient for a simple stabbing, but the left side would have been more certain but more difficult to access the heart which is sloped slight away to the left in the Pericardial Cavity."

McNab tried to follow his friends reasoning by imagining the students' hurried departure up the aisle and past the second last row of seats.

"No, the murderer must have been one of the last to leave and been at the end of the queue of departing students. Do you see my reasoning?" the spirit said with a look of confidence on his grey face.

"Ummm..yes. That seems most logical." McNab stammered. But why kill him here in a relatively public place?"

"Opportunity, my boy. The stabbing would have been very quick and, had not the porter been nearby to restore the room, our murderer could have also removed the body. All he had to do was wait until all of the students had cleared the corridor, put the body on one of the trolleys outside and then taken it down to the Cadaver Room. There, he would have removed all of its clothing and belongings and attached a label to its big toe and presto! Just another cadaver. Simple, really."

"But then the plan was interrupted!" McNab added enthusiastically. "The porter arrived, so our murderer had to go out with the rest of the students and lurk somewhere until the horrified Porter ran off to alert the authorities. Then he would have taken the body downstairs, as you suggest, but knowing that the place would soon be crawling with police, he panicked and stuff the body into a convenient cabinet without getting very far with the undressing and preparing the new cadaver."

"Exactly, my boy! You are starting to think like a detective!"

"But there are still two problems with which I am puzzled." McNab said, looking up exquisitely at his friend. "Where did his mobile phone go? And why was he killed in the first place?"

"Och!" said the spirit with a look of disgust on his face. "Yes, I have seen these foolish devices which the students all seem to have their noses in. They seem to have them out at all times of day." The spirit brought the open palm of his hand close up to his nose in imitation of using a mobile phone. "If we assume that this poor soul had one in his hand, he would have dropped it when he was killed and I would also suggest that his killer would have quickly picked it up on his way out of the door. It certainly was not on the body when you searched it. As to motive? Well! That is a complex matter." The spirit sat down and turned towards the front of the lecture room. Then he suddenly spun around with a gleam in his eye.

"Why of course! A little bit fanciful but it might just be the reason!" He jumped up and glided quickly out of the rear door calling back as he did so. "Follow me. We go back down to the Cadaver Room."

McNab also jumped up and followed the spirit as he glided down the corridor and then down the stairwell to the basement of the deserted building. At the locked door of the Cadaver Room, which also had a mass of blue and white checked tape criss-cross it, the spirit went through the adjoining wall and again unlocked the door from the inside. McNab crawled on his hands and knees beneath the tape and then stood up in the chill of the long room.

The spirit turned back to face McNab and said with that unmistakeable gleam in his eye: "Now, we only looked into some of these nearest cabinets did we not? The first containing a standard cadaver, the others being empty and the last one we tried, containing our dressed-up victim."

"Why yes!" said the now confused young detective.

"Well, here is the first cabinet containing our standard cadaver. Open it and turn the body over. I think that you might find two unstitched incisions in its lower dorsal section."

McNab had some difficulty turning the body over; a dead weight in many sense of the term. When the body finally flopped onto its chest, McNab was amazed to find that there were indeed two long incisions now blue and open in both sides of its lower back. He looked up at the spirit who had glided down to another set of three stacked cabinets.

"Let us now open several of these and find others with the same condition."
McNab, opened several which proved to be empty and then a lower cabinet which contained a cadaver. He again rolled it over but did not find the same marks on its back as before. Disappointed he tried the next cabinet with the same result. He went down the line of

cabinets and after considerable effort found three other cadavers with the marks on their backs. "What does all of this mean, Dr Bell? What are these marks?"

The spirit stood back and folded his arms and a broad grin lit up his usually sombre face. "Well, I thought of something which was somewhat of a well-known legend when I was a young medical student here back in the 1850's. Not too much earlier than that, I think that it was about 1828 or so, there had been a great scandal in the Anatomy Department, here in this very university. There had been two serial killers in Edinburgh by the names of William Burke and William Hare. Have you heard of these two unworthies, detective?"

McNab replied, "Why yes, Dr. Bell. Weren't they the inspiration for Robert Louis Stevenson's novel *The Body Snatchers*?"

"Indeed, my boy. The two men were active in Edinburgh between 1827 and 1828 and they famously sold their victims' bodies to a Dr Robert Knox. He was an influential lecturer in our Anatomy Department where he and his colleagues dissected the bodies as part of their anatomical research. You must remember that they did not have the luxury of donated corpses in those days, but relied on the acquisition of bodies of prisoners, suicides and the like. Burke and Hare started out in their grisly trade by simply digging up freshly buried corpses, but soon demand exceeded supply. They then decided to 'cut out the middle man' as they say, and get their fresh bodies through murder. Sounds similar to our case?"

McNab looked at the spirit with some uncertainty: "But what are these incisions in the cadavers here?"

"Think, laddie! Does the medical school need to steal bodies today? No! But there is a great need for the kidneys of bodies, is there not?"

McNab looked at the back of the last cadaver and of the two scars running down the sides of its back. There had been prolific media coverage recently about the long waiting lists for kidney transplants in the United Kingdom. In places overseas, kidneys could be legally sold by their donors, but in most countries, those with kidney disease could only receive the organs from living volunteer donors or from the recently deceased who's will allowed for their organs to be donated. There was, unfortunately also a 'black market' in kidneys for those who did not wish to wait in the long queue. Even here in the United Kingdom, such transactions existed.

The spirit walked over to the opposite side of the cadaver on the tray. "Now, laddie. It would not be too unthinkable to have a senior student with the elements of surgical removal to do such a thing. All they would need would be to have access to this room, their skill and some illegal or unsuspecting contact with various hospitals. It would be quite feasible to supply those needy but impatient individuals with a kidney or two under the guise of a sudden donation from this august institution. The money would only change hands between the agent here and the person needing the operation or a relative. The hospital may not even know about the 'finer details' shall we say, of the donation."

McNab scratched his head: "Yes, but wouldn't the absent of kidneys here in the cadavers be detected when the depleted bodies were brought up for student dissections?"

The spirit looked troubled and stroked his chin. "You have a point there, detective. I suppose that such removal could be blamed on a previous student dissection, but as there are only a few in that state it might not be too difficult to explain. Remember that sometimes, like that last lecture, not all of the cadaver is used."

"So how would such a trade include our murder victim?" McNab asked.

The spirit had now gone almost completely transparent; an act which also seemed to occur when he was perplexed or annoyed: "Perhaps he was also a senior student here with access to the Cadaver Room and found out and was going on. If he threatened to divulge the name of culprit then there would be a need for him to be removed. That is just an hypothesis, mind and a difficult one for me to think about."

With that, the spirit disappeared in a trail of blue smoke leaving the young detective alone in the darkened room to think of the many possibilities for a motive.

4.

The next morning, McNab sat at his cluttered desk in his little corner and looked through the long list of names which the Medical School secretary had reluctantly given him. He had counted eighty-seven names of which seventy-five were listed as students. The rest were possibly members of the general public or staff and unlike the students' names, there were no other details listed. Simon Elliott's name was not listed at all and who knows how many other attendees were also anonymous. Of the seventy-five students listed, sixty-one were students in their senior years; from their third to their sixth year of medical studies. Whilst most had their contact details listed, usually only a mobile phone number, some did not. These potential suspects were going to be very hard to locate and interview. McNab put the list down and stood up.

Across the big room of cluttered desks, he could see that Olivia Kerr's desk was unoccupied leaving him feeling even more depressed.

He looked down at the wallet which he had taken from the murder victim. At least he had a name, even if it did not show up on the list of attendees at the lecture. He hoped that DS Kerr would have better luck when she interviewed the bank manager at the Nicolson Street Branch of the Royal Bank of Scotland.

With a little hope, he turned to his computer and opened his ProLinkNet account which he hoped would provide some additional professional occupations of the victim and the named suspects. In its search box, he typed the name of Simon Elliott and waited. There were over eight-hundred responses. Bother! He narrowed down the search by putting 'Edinburgh' after the name; assuming that the victim was in fact a local. A slim chance. There were now only fifty-nine responses for that name. This was going to take some time.

It was well after lunch when Olivia Kerr came into the office. She strode over to McNab's desk and sat down on its edge looking confident with herself.

McNab had been half asleep but suddenly sat up and blinked.

"Hamish! I have been and I have conquered!" she said with a smile. I have Mr. Elliott's mobile phone number which the bank manager read from his account details so we may be able to locate his mobile phone and possibly the killer if he still has it."

McNab looked up and said joyfully. "Why, that's wonderful, DS Kerr…I mean Olivia. I have not found any professional details about our victim. I was hoping that he would be a doctor, student or even a medical administrator in…"

Before he could continue, DS Kerr interrupted: "…the Lothian Private Hospital!" McNab looked into her smiling face and grinned. She continued:

"And that piece of paper with the numbers? It proved to be an account under the name of John Anderson. The manager filled me with a lot of banking jargon, trying to impress this 'dumb blonde' but I got answers to all of my questions never-the-less. He even condescended to have copies of the bank statements printed out for the accounts of Mr. Simon Elliott and Mr. John Anderson. Here you are." She handed several pieces of paper to McNab.

She continued whilst pointing her finger at the sheets of paper." You will also notice that over the year, our dead Mr. Elliott had received several large, identical payments each of thirty thousand pounds. Moreover, if you look closely at the dates of these payments, this Mr. John Anderson has also about the same time received identical payments of twenty thousand pounds from Elliott's bank account."

McNab told her about the possible motive for the victim's death, neglecting to mention that it had come from Bell's story."

DS Kerr gave a short whistle and said, "Thirty thousand pounds! A lot of money for a poor hospital administrator, but still a cheap price for an illegal kidney. It looks like our victim was getting a nice profit of ten thousand dollars." She turned the last page of Anderson's bank account and pointed to near the bottom of the page. "But look at the last figure paid to procurer Anderson – only fifteen thousand pounds this time. It looks like Elliott wanted a bigger slice of the kidney pie and Anderson probably resented the cut in his profits. Done! Motive established!"

McNab looked at the dates corresponding to the transfer of the large amounts of money and smiled. "Well done, Olivia! We now know that Elliott and Anderson were in the illegal organ business with Anderson being the man at the Medical School who removed the kidneys from donated cadavers and passed them on to Elliott who was perhaps the 'brains' of the operation. He obviously had the criminal connections which made it known that his hospital is where wealthy and impatient patients could jump the transplant queue if they paid the appropriate price. As the Administrator there, he probably was in charge of legal donor organ procurement as well and would also have been in charge of the details and thus preferential selection the recipients of the illegal kidneys."

"A smooth operation, if I can use a sick pun?" Olivia replied, "and Anderson here at the Medical School would probably have had access to the Cadaver Room and would be able to remove kidneys on demand. They could have then been legally sent by courier in chilled containers with the Medical Schools imprimatur ready for the transplant. I think that a kidney can last up to thirty-six hours out of the body, there would have plenty of access time. But who was he, this John Anderson? A student? A member of staff? Who?"

They both looked at each other and almost simultaneously cried out aloud: "Iain McAndrew!"

"Yes!" cried McNab, shooting a clenched fist into the air. "Exactly! 'John Anderson' is the Anglicised form of 'Iain McAndrew'. Got you!"

"Good work, Hamish!" cried Olivia. "He's our man! As the person in charge of the Cadaver Room, he would have full access to it at all times as well as the school's emergency courier service. Shall I send a couple of the uniform lads over to bring him in?"

"No! There's still some additional evidence that I may be able to get for our prosecution. If you wish, let's get the uniform lads by all means and drive over to the Medical School so that I can speak to our Dr. McAndrew."

It being only a short distance between the station and the Medical School, the police car pulled up at the kerb near the imposing arch and its four occupants, McNab, Kerr and two uniformed officers, walked through the archway, across the courtyard and into the reception area. The strait-laced secretary looked up in surprise and this time, McNab was in a more aggressive mood:

"Where is Dr. McAndrew's office, please?" he said in a deep, confident voice, showing his detective's identification. The startled secretary looked at the two uniformed officers standing behind the two detectives and stammered:

"Just down the corridor to your right and around the corner of the building." She said meekly, pointing the way.

Just upstairs from the basement Cadaver Room, McNab thought as he turned and led the way along the corridor. When they reached a small door, which bore the name 'Dr. McAndrew, Chief Demonstrator', McNab turned to Olivia and gave her a small piece of paper with a mobile telephone number on it. "Give me five minutes inside alone and then ring this number. It belongs to Elliott's missing mobile phone. If McAndrew is as naïve a criminal as I think that he is, he will probably have the mobile in his office somewhere." With that, he knocked on the door and entered without waiting for a reply.

A startled young man sat at a desk on the opposite side of what appeared to be a rather untidy room. "Who the devil are you?" he said, jumping to his feet revealing a tall, well-built body more suited to the rough and tumble of a football field than a medical school.

McNab quickly walked over to the front of the desk and showed him his identification. McAndrew sat down, his face now white and he ran his fingers through his sparce black hair. "What do you want?" he weakly asked.

McNab was right about the man's criminal professionalism. Here was as frightened an amateur criminal if he ever saw one. Standing, McNab revised the events of the previous day and the murder of Simon Elliott at the end of the lecture. He put it to the young demonstrator that he had followed the students up the steps in the lecture room and in the usual confusion of their departure had killed Elliott with the scalpel he had used during the dissection.

Suddenly, there was a muffled ringtone from one of the drawers in McAndrew's desk.

"Mr. Elliott calling, I believe, Dr. McAndrew!" McNab said placing both hands down onto the desk. McAndrew sprang from around the desk knocking McNab to the floor and ran across the room, exiting through the open door which he slammed shut behind him. McNab sat up and heard a loud crash from outside.

Dashing to the door, he opened it to find McAndrew's body crumpled up against the wall. Olivia was rubbing her hands together but with a satisfied look on her face; the two constables both had broad grins on their faces.

"Always thought that being a First Kyu Jishukan Ryu would one day be useful in my profession!" she said looking up into McNab's startled face. "That's Senior Brown Belt in mixed martial arts to you, Hamish."

Turning to the constables she said: "Cuff this creep and let's get him back to the station for charging with murder." She looked back at McNab who was still standing with his mouth open. "Looks like your phone ploy worked. You had better retrieve it from the office, but don't get your fingerprints on it!".

That evening, McNab sat on the second bottom step of the darkened lecture room in the Old medical School and waited for his friend. Soon there was the usual wisp of blue luminous smoke and the ghost of Dr. Joseph Bell slowly appeared. The spirit walked down onto the floor of the lecture room and turned when he got to the long bench at its front.

"So, my young detective. I perceive that as you look rather happy with yourself, that you have learnt from my little lessons in deduction and have solved the crime. Am I right?"

"Yes, thank you, Dr. Bell. I could not have done it without your help. It was the Demonstrator

McAndrew who killed his greedy partner in their little kidney business just as you suggested."

The spirit held up both arms in a show of satisfaction and then folded them across his chest. "No trouble at all my boy. I am glad that there was a satisfactory conclusion and that I might have been able to teach you a few things about deductive reasoning. So, tell me all about the details of your methodology."

McNab stood up and walked across the lecture room floor and sat up on the bench. He briefly outlined the facts of the case; the roles of McAndrew and of the late Simon Elliott. The deductions of Dr. Bell which had led to the final arrest. He did not, however tell the spirit about his new happy relationship with DS Olivia Kerr and of the personal feeling of satisfaction about the respect now paid to him at the station by its Chief Inspector and the other detectives.

The spirit looked pleased with himself and with the results of McNab's ability to learn from him. "You can call on me if you ever need some further assistance, my young detective. There is still much that you could learn from this old spirit, but remember that we…umm spirits if you like to call us by that term, are neither omnipotent nor omnipresent. We come and go when we feel like it and are not everywhere at once. When I come down to one of my usual haunts in your dimension, it usually takes considerable energy out of me for a while. This is why you feel the temperature drop when I arrive. But as you have seen, there are some advantages of being dead. Here, take my hand." With that, the spirit extended a thin, white hand which McNab took. It was very cold to the touch but the grip was firm. McNab felt a tingling pass through his hand, up his arm and into the rest of the body. He shivered.

"There! That wasn't too bad was it?" The spirit said. "We are now bonded as it were. If you ever need my services again, you no longer have to come into this creepy old lecture room. Just go somewhere quiet; preferably anywhere which is dark and likely not to receive any interruption and just call my name."

With that last comment, Dr. Bell slowly faded into the familiar wisp of blue smoke, a smile lasting on his intelligent face.

The Lone Piper

1.

It was a chilly Saturday night in August and a light breeze was blowing from Arthur's Seat down onto the Esplanade of Edinburgh Castle. Hamish McNab, now a full Detective Constable, sat in the cheap seats high up in the temporary grandstand nearest the wall of the castle itself. The cold breeze was blowing onto his face but he did not mind; he was sitting next to Detective Sergeant Olivia Kerr; perhaps the best-looking detective in all of Scotland. He had summoned up enormous courage, those many weeks ago and had asked her if she would like to be his guest at the forthcoming Edinburgh Military Tattoo; that annual spectacle which drew local crowds and tourists from all over the world. He was amazed, and greatly delighted, when she had readily accepted his invitation with that subtle smile which he had come to appreciate. McNab had always been a shy person and also had reservations about socialising with a colleague, but he had come to like this beautiful and capable woman who had a well-founded reputation at the station for being a very smart detective.

They had enjoyed the evening; the various marching bands from home and abroad, especially the energetic Army Band from New Zealand who performed a stirring Maori Haka. They had even shared in the joke when a visiting American tourist, complete with camera and loud checked coat, had complained about the state of the Scottish weather:

"Ah don't thank much uh o' yur goddam Scottish Summer!" he had exclaimed rather too loudly than good taste would allow.

This had induced a nearby local wit to reply: "Och aye. Gin it gets any hotter, a'll have tae tak ma vest aff!"

The last individual act of the night had just marched off when the lights slowly dimmed and the lone piper high up on the walls of the Half Moon Battery was illuminated with a narrow spotlight. Most of the crowd hushed, but the American and his friends continued to talk in their loud southern drawl about the weather and the superior skills of the American Drill Team which had been one of earlier guest acts. The piper, usually one of the best in the army, played the lament *Sleep, Dearie, Sleep* and McNab felt the hairs on the back of his head rise with emotion. As soon as it had finished and the lights came back on, Olivia leaned over and said in a knowing way:

"You know, there's an interesting legend about the Lone Piper. Do you want to hear it?"

She was interrupted by the loud voice of the Tattoo Master of Ceremonies who now announced that the assembled bands, drill teams and other guests would now assemble and march off to the stirring tune of *The Black Bear*. There now could be no competition with such a rousing tune so Olivia left her story until later as the rest of the crowd clapped their hands loudly in unison to the drums and pipes. To the stirring tune, the assembled multitude marched back up the Esplanade before crossing the narrow stone bridge into the castle. Olivia had clapped her hands over her ears and gave McNab a smiling grimace. She had commented earlier in the night that she thought that even though she was a good Scot, she did not enjoy the music of the pipes. To her ears, the bagpipes sounded too much like a cat being tortured. McNab had made some half-hearted comment that such a sentiment was typical of a Border clan but was quickly rebuked that her dislike was one of personal taste, and not one shared by Clan Kerr nor any other Lowlander. McNab had always thrilled to the sound of the pipes as did his family who had come from the Highlands. His parents had moved down from the Highlands after the war, but many of his uncles still resided in the little village of Killin in Perthshire.

Finally, the last of the mass pipes and drums and their guests had marched across the narrow stone bridge and into the gatehouse of the castle. The MC wished everyone a "goodnight and a safe journey home" as all of the lights around the Esplanade came on. As the crowd began to push their way down from the temporary grandstands onto the security of the flat stone pavement below, McNab turned to his friend and asked:

"So! What is this great legend of yours?"

"As I was about to say," she said, "there's an interesting legend about the Lone Piper. I'll tell it to you whilst we wait for the crowd to thin a little".

"Why not?" McNab replied. Olivia had been relatively quiet all evening so he encouraged her to talk about herself more freely. She pointed up to where the lone piper had been playing his lament.

"They say that on the Half Moon Battery, where our lone piper played tonight, some soldiers a long time ago and late at night, found some hidden steps leading down to a deep tunnel which headed off underground below the Esplanade and then under the Royal Mile."

McNab looked at her with an uncertain sideways glance: "Oh, I'm sure." He said cynically. "There are supposed to be tunnels all under the castle."

"Well, then." she continued," they dragged a poor piper, or some say he was a drummer boy, out of his barracks bunk and made him play as they pushed him down the steps and into the tunnel. They had decided to find out where this tunnel went by following the sounds of the pipes coming up from below as they walked across the Esplanade and into the Royal Mile. They could hear the quiet, muffled sounds of the pipes coming up from the tunnel below as they walked. But..." Here, she paused for her dramatic ending.

"Go on, please." McNab said with some encouragement.

"...suddenly, the music stopped and when the bravest of them followed the boy into the tunnel he came to a stone wall blocking the tunnel and they never saw the young piper ever again. However, many people since then have claimed to hear the muffled sounds of the pipes late at night from the empty battlements. They say that the Tattoo's lone piper now plays a lament at the end of the show in honour of the small boy piper who never returned."

McNab looked at her with all innocence and said: "Oh! That's interesting. I always thought that the Tattoo's lone piper was playing the lament traditionally used at the end of the day to recall the troops to their bed and 'lights out'. Scottish regiments all over the world still do that every night!"

"You're right, of course," she said with a sigh. "It's just another ghost story to scare little children. Even though the castle is said to be haunted by many ghosts, we both know that there are no such things as ghosties and ghoulies."

"Well, it's an interesting story, never-the-less." McNab said turning away to hide his smile. "Now, the crowd has thinned so let's get back to your car."

He helped her down from the tiered grandstand and walked by her side as they followed the crowd down the slope of the Esplanade and into the Royal Mile. They passed under the temporary gate at the end of the Esplanade and passed by the Witches Well, that small monument to accused witches who had been burnt at the stake in Edinburgh many centuries past. They turned into the small entrance to the narrow Ramsay Lane which led steeply downhill to The Mound and then across the railway lines to Princes Street, the busiest street of the city.

At Princes Street, they turned left and walked along the almost deserted road and turned into Queensferry Street at the small square where it intersected with Hope Street. As they had been to the later session of the Tattoo it was now rather late at night and there were few people about when they finally turned into Alva Street where Olivia had parked her small car.

They had only walked a short distance along the darkened street with its fashionable Georgian buildings when they came to her car. Olivia was just about to open its door when they heard a belligerent voice behind them:

"Well, nah! whit have we here? a nice couple comin' 'ome from the tattoo, hey?"

They both turned and saw that the voice came from a large skinhead standing in front of three of his shorter cronies. He wore a grubby kilt of some indeterminable clan held up with a pair of braces over an even grubbier sleeveless pullover. There were tattoos – the skin variety – over most of his thick arms and sides of his head which was topped with a narrow hedgerow of red hair. McNab had had only a fleeting experience with some of the tough youths of the inner city; his uniformed duties had been mostly involved with crowd control at football matches at Tynecastle Stadium or walking the local park during the day. He quickly pulled his Identification Badge from his coat pocket and said with as much conviction as he could muster: "We're police!"

The big skinhead gave a look of mock terror, turning to his cronies, and replied with a broad grin: "Och aye now! It's tha' Polis com tey huckle us, lads wi' his luvly mot." The cronies all laughed.

A short, fat skinhead emerged from behind his big leader and said with a scowl: "Ah hate tha Polis!" and drew an ugly looking knife from the big leather belt which held up his kilt and stomach.

The big skinhead advanced towards Olivia. "Yer mot's a pretty lassie, aint she?" he said reaching out one big arm.

Olivia simply smiled, took one long step backward with her right leg then brought it and the hard leather heel of her sensibly sturdy shoe quickly up, striking the skinhead's chin in a snap kick. "Mae Geri Keage!" she yelled, naming the type of kick used, as was the habit back at her martial arts dojo. The big skinhead's head snapped back and the rest of his body followed it to the pavement.

There was a stunned "Gawd!" from the cronies, but the fat skinhead came at McNab with his knife in his outstretched hand. McNab quickly remembered his Uncle Coinneach McNab's advice when he first joined the force, "Whan a Ned comes tae ye wi a knife, dinnae wist time tryin tae disarm the bastard - juist kick him i the goolies!" Which is exactly what he did. Without a sporran to protect his assets, the fat skinhead bent over with a loud grown clutching his groin. To help him on his way down, McNab used his forehead to add a 'Glasgow kiss' to that of his assailant.

The other two skinheads, seeing the quick demise of their two friends, turned and ran off down the street. Olivia straightened her jacket and unlocked the door to her car. She turned to McNab and said with a sweet smile: "Thank you for the lovely evening, Hamish. It has been a most entertaining night and with some extra training value tossed in. I'll see you at the station on Monday." With that, she stepped over the inert body of the big skinhead and leant over and gave

McNab a little kiss on his forehead. "There! That'll make your poor head better. Good night."

2.

The stirring sound of the marching pipe band resonated through the narrow canyon of the ancient grey-brown stone buildings of the Royal Mile. The Eight Battalion (Army Reserve) marched with a strong, strident gait down the slope to the tune of *Scotland the Brave*; their green fighting kilts swinging with the skirl of the pipes. The red jackets and black bearskins of the pipes and drums behind the imposing Drum Major gave some added colour to the spectacle.

The spectators, who stood back against the old stone walls to let them past, could only stand and watch with admiration and pride. Behind the band came the main body of the Battalion in their dark green kilts, jackets and Glengarry bonnets; led by their Colonel and his officers followed by the guard and then the Colour Party. This was a ceremonial Church Parade so that the Colours could be laid up, albeit temporarily during their annual training, in the old St. Giles' Cathedral further down the Royal Mile.

The band marched proudly, its youngest officers trying to hold up the Battalion's Colours in the cold, icy wind blowing down the narrow confines of the Lawnmarket. It was a cold morning and the first dusting of snow lay upon Arthur's Seat which brooded over the city. The Eighth Battalion now marched to have their Colours blessed in the High Kirk on the Royal Mile; it was to be a highlight of their brief stay at the castle. Being a Reserve unit, they had been given the honour of garrisoning the castle during this, their Annual Training period. At the end of the month, they would once again return to their barracks in the west of the city from where they would again disperse to their various humdrum civilian occupations.

But today, they marched proudly as a Scottish regiment should: proud men and women with smiles on their faces. Well, not all. They had left two of their number back at the castle; excused from Church Parade and given the honour of guarding the main gate in the cold and the light snow which had started to fall. The other person who was not happy was the battalion's Adjutant, Captain Thomas Payne. Payne had come from a very well-known English regiment of the regular army noted for its tough professionalism and secret operations during wartime. Payne was a professional soldier and felt very unhappy at having being suddenly posted, against all of his personal complaints, to a Reserve Army battalion; and a Scottish one at that! The wearing of a kilt and bonnet was totally foreign to him and he felt undressed out of his usual khaki Service Dress. He felt no love for this battalion and the men and women in it, and he knew that this hostile feeling was reciprocated.

So, Adjutant Captain Thomas Payne marched independently along the side of the marching body of troops and found fault after fault with his citizen soldier. He certainly would be having a word with Regimental Sergeant-Major McInnes when the parade was over and prescribing some new form of drill or extreme activity to show his displeasure.

"Battal'on will right wheel!" ordered Regimental Sergeant-Major McInnes whose stentorian voice could probably be heard back at the castle. The column wheeled expertly around to the right and followed the band and the Colours through the now opened barricade of chains that marked out the small square in front of the kirk. They marched past the statue of the Duke of Buccleuch until all of the main body had entered the square.

"Battal'on halt! Left turn! Order Arms. Stand at ease!" the RSM called in perfect time for each movement. At his next command, "Duty Men as ordered will fall out!" Two soldiers in the front rank, answered 'Sar, Major', came to attention, and holding their rifles at the trail, left the ranks and walked smartly up the stone steps and into the imposing entrance to the kirk.

Sergeant-Major McInnes watched the two soldiers go and then turned back to the main body and, in his loud voice barked out the next order: "Battal'on Attention!" There was a dull sound of many boots being brought together and then silence. The words of command came again in the crisp air: "On the command 'Fall Out', front rank leading, you will remove your bonnets and will follow the officers and Colours into the kirk and fill up from the front on alternative sides. You will walk – not march – and watch out for them rifles on the woodwork you heath'n people." A quiet ripple of laughter went through the ranks following this last remark, as Sergeant-Major McInnes was well-liked as well as being well-respected as a former Regular soldier.

Back at the station, McNab looked out over his little corner desk and through the smudged window panes of the big office with its clutter of myriad desks. It was almost Christmas in Edinburgh and a light fall of snow had put a white dusting over the grey slates of the city's rooves. "It was going to be a cold winter." He thought as he continued with the mundane reports on the cases he had attended over the last few months; two thefts in the High Street; several muggings in Leith and a home invasion in Morningside. These were nothing much to tax his ability and confidence but he was feeling a bit down on this cold, grey morning. This was probably because DS Kerr had been absent for over a week, being attached to Glasgow police to assist with a case of fraud in one of the most well-known insurance companies.

It was with some relief when DCI MacFarlane, the Head of the CID at the station, came up to his desk later that morning. He looked concerned and McNab, still remembering his days, not so long ago, as a uniformed Constable jumped to his feet.

"Oh, sit down, McNab!" MacFarlane said with a little irritation. "A major issue has just occurred which will require all of your powers as an investigative detective." McNab sat down and tried to look as intelligent as he could as his chief continued: "It's a terrible bleak day to be out, to be certain, but a passer-by walking their dog along Johnston Terrace has just reported that they have seen a body in the snow. It apparently lies on the rocky slope below the Half

Moon Battery of the castle. Get a team out there and do what you can."

McNab quickly called for two of the uniform officers and alerted the forensic team by telephone. On arriving at the scene, they parked their small car in the Bus Zone in Johnson Terrace just below the castle walls and with some difficulty, climbed over the small, spiked fence at the start of the small lane which ran around the base of the castle rock. It wasn't a difficult climb up the small turf and rock slope which went up steeply to the very wall of the Half Moon Battery. Right in the corner where the Battery's wall adjoined the vertical cliff below the Great Hall, they found the body covered over with a light dusting of snow.

McNab sent the two officers back down the slope to control the small crowd of tourists who had just arrived in a big blue coach whilst he examined the body which was lying on its back and partly arched over a jutting piece of rock.

He had been a soldier; the three pips on each of his epaulettes showed him to be a Captain in the now crumpled kilt of the Eighth Battalion (Army Reserve). McNab reached into the body's top left hand jacket pocket and pulled out the soldier's Parade Card. The name on the card read 'Thomas Payne' and as the paper of the card was relatively new, McNab reasoned that this Captain Payne had only recently joined the unit. He felt some pride with his observations from his previous lessons with the ghost Dr. Bell. They had given him some new confidence in the skills of deductive reasoning. "Well, now, Dr. Bell, what do you think of that?" he said quietly to himself. He looked more closely at the limp body more closely; there was blood seeping out from underneath the body as well as multiple wounds on its face and chest. McNab looked up and judged that the victim had fallen from the parapet above; a distance of about twelve metres. A direct drop of this distance onto the sloping turf may not have been fatal, but a small piece of green uniform on a sharp pinnacle of rock jutting out from the cliff just above the slope suggested otherwise.

McNab jumped up suddenly when he heard that familiar voice just next to his ear. "Look to its head, Laddie. You'll see that there is a wound on the back of the head which has long ago congealed. Compare that to the blood which has seeped across the rock below the body. It has not yet formed a crust. What do you think of that, now?"

McNab looked around but could not see his friend, Dr. Bell. The voice laughed and said: "Och, now! You'll not be wanting yon police officers and the gawking crowd to see me, do you now?"

"No! Certainly not, Dr. Bell."

"Now, what about this head wound, then?" the spirit continued.

McNab looked again at the body. "The wet blood on the rock suggests that he hasn't been here very long." McNab also remembered his friend's demonstrations back at the Old medical School and lifted up a limp arm and let it fall back again. "Rigor Mortis has not fully set in, so he has probably been here under about two hours, even with the cold."

"Excellent, Laddie!" The spirit voice laughed; "But what about the wound on the back of the head? Congealed blood, mind."

McNab turned the head around and looked at the long gash on the rear and top of the victim's head: "The congealed blood suggests that the head wound was made before the fall; most likely he was bashed with a heavy object. One with a sharp edge judging from the width and length of the wound."

A laugh came from the invisible spirit. "Och! You're becoming a wonderful detective. Exactly! Good observation and deduction. Have you noticed anything else?"

McNab looked off into the distance where he thought that the spirit may be standing. "Well, yes! His Parade Card is relatively new, so I would think that he has recently joined the unit and he was Captain Thomas Payne."

"Good work, laddie. Now, look at his campaign ribbons above his pocket on the left-hand side of his jacket. They seem impressive and shows an officer with much experience. I am not up on current military history, but I would suggest that he has seen active overseas service in the Regular Army, even if he wears the uniform of a local Territorial unit."

"Yes, of course Dr. Bell. Now that is a puzzling thing, but we now call the 'Territorials' the 'Army Reserve'."

"Och! No matter! He is a very experienced Captain in the…. Reserves is it? So, he is most likely not a simple

Captain in charge of a Company. As a former Regular, he most likely is the unit's Adjutant."

"I understand." Said McNab. "I was briefly in the Reserves myself for two years and we had an Adjutant who was posted from the Regs. He generally was an overseer and guide for our training and helped with the paperwork which the army loved to send in copious amounts. We did not see him too often as he tended to keep himself in HQ and only appeared at parades or when something went wrong."

"Well enough!" said the voice nearby. "So, it looks like our poor Adjutant, Captain Payne was knocked on the head and thrown over yon parapet above. It looks like he might have been unpopular or had found something he should not have found. Wait...I'll be back." And then there was silence.

It was only a minute or two when the voice returned. "I've just had a wee look up on yon battlements. Nothing suspicious there and I noticed that the Battery was totally empty even with a goodly crowd of visitors down below going through the main gate. The Battery, you ken, is out of the way. Any visitor has to walk up the long slope away from and well below the Battery itself to get to the main parts of the castle. I'm not surprised that the Battery is unoccupied and judging from the few marks in the new snow, it has not been visited by too many people this morning."

"Are there any footsteps like up there?" McNab asked.

"Good question, laddie! Yes, there are some marks on the pavement up there, but they are not very distinct. Remember that the light fall of snow has only occurred this morning so this also puts the fall of the body to a recent time. The marks up there also suggest no more than two or three people and there are also some marks suggesting that something has been dragged; our Captain Payne perhaps. It is interesting, though, that the marks did not seem to come from further down the slope leading to the battery, but were only made not far from the parapet itself. Most interesting!"

"Hello up there" came a voice from below and McNab turned to see the two forensic men climbing over the corner of the railing near the street.

"I'll be off then." said the voice at McNab's ear as the two men clambered up the slope towards him and the body. When they got there, McNab gave them his findings; supplemented by those from Dr. Bell:

"This is the body is of Captain Thomas Payne, the recently attached Adjutant of the Eighth Battalion. It appears that he was knocked unconscious by a heavy but sharp object and then thrown over the parapet above. You will notice that his multiple wounds and bone fractures are relatively new and that the time of death was probably just at the first fall of snow this morning."

The Forensic Team, the same two men who had attended McNab's last murder case at the Old medical School, again looked at the young detective with some awe.

McNab left the scene of the crime walking up the long slope of Johnson Terrace to the steep steps of Castle Wynd North which led directly to the Esplanade and the castle.

Walking up the Esplanade, he came to the narrow stone bridge which went across the dry moat into the Gatehouse. On either side of the stone bridge and set a little way from its entrance, where two tall wooden sentry boxes complete with sentries gazing far afield both in the uniform of the Eighth Battalion (Army Reserve). Both soldiers where in the 'at ease' position with their rifles down by their right sides; the soldier on the right-hand-side bore the single chevron of a Lance Corporal. McNab walked up to him and displayed his identification.

"Where can I find the Commanding Officer, please?" he asked. The soldier came to attention and looked directly at McNab. "In the Officers' Mess, ah wad assum Sir, as our unit has juist come from Church Parade. Gae throuch the gatehouse, turn richt an follow the main path throuch the archway an up the ro'd. The Officers' Mess is i the old Governor's House. Sir!" The soldier again assumed the 'attention' position again looking straight ahead. Conversation over.

McNab thanked him and walked across the narrow bridge into the castle. Coming out from the Gatehouse, he turned right as instructed and followed the path up through the tunnel of the Argyle Tower and past the Mills Point Battery where the One O'clock Gun is now fired.

Across the small square near where the pathway curved up to the left, he saw the imposing three-story building with its prominent arched doorway; the old Governor's House. McNab walked up the few steps and opened the single, dark brown door. He was soon greeted in the anteroom by a young officer still in his marching uniform and was informed that the

Commanding Officer had only just returned to his office which was conveniently just down the long corridor. McNab followed the officer's directions and walked into a large room which had two desks; the larger of the two, he noticed, was unoccupied and had a nameplate labelled 'ADJUTANT". The other was occupied by the Duty Orderly, a Corporal, who looked up and asked:

"Can ah help ye, sir?"

McNab showed the orderly his identification and asked to see the Colonel of the Battalion. The orderly stood up and walked to a closed door just past the Adjutant's desk. He knocked, entered and then looked back at McNab, holding the door open:

"Colonel McDonald will see ye now, sir," he said, standing aside so that McNab could enter and then closed the door after him. A thick set man in his middle years with silver hair stood up from behind his desk and came round to meet the detective. He had a friendly smile on his sunburnt face and he extended his hand out to McNab:

"I'm Colonel Andrew McDonald. I suppose your visit is about our missing Adjutant, Captain Payne. Is it not?" McNab thought that news certainly travels fast here in Edinburgh. "Your Headquarters has only just telephoned me about his body. Nasty business. Please have a seat." He gestured to a small chair in front of the big desk then returned to his own chair on the other side.

McNab sat down and asked the Colonel about the dead Adjutant and of his movements during the morning's Church Parade. The Colonel placed his big hand upon the desk and looked at McNab with sad eyes:

"Captain Payne was sent to us only two weeks ago from one of the most illustrious fighting units of the Regular Army. Apparently, he had become somewhat of an outcast in his own regiment due to a scandal –

the nature of which I will not go into. Anyway, he was very unhappy at being posted to a reserve unit such as ourselves and his training of my soldiers was at times very hard for civilian volunteers; such as extra drill early in the morning, debussing out of trucks at speed and so on."

McNab looked at the Colonel with some sympathy: "I can imagine, Colonel. I had two years in the Reserves myself and some mornings were very difficult to handle; especially in winter."

"Quite so, detective. As to his mental health, I must say that Captain Payne was a troubled man with a considerable amount of personal shame, so it comes as no great surprise to me that he would want to end his own life."

McNab looked down at the desk and then back at Colonel McDonald: "I'm afraid that I believe that poor Captain Payne may have had some unrequested help in the matter of going over the parapet."

Colonel McDonald looked shocked at this revelation: "Good Lord! Do you mean to say that Captain Payne was murdered?"

"Most likely, Colonel. Did he have any enemies in the Battalion?"

"Well, he certainly did not have any friends here! I did the best I could to help him adjust to our casual way of soldering, but he was a hard man to get to know and kept himself at a distance from all of the other officers. The soldiers, I believed, generally hated him for his antagonism and arrogant personality. I hardly think, however that anyone in the entire Battalion would want to do away with him, especially on our doorstep as it were."

"Thank you, Colonel. What were Captain Payne's movements this morning?" McNab said, taking his small notebook out of the top pocket of his coat.

The Colonel leant back in his chair and looked up at the ceiling: "Well, now! let me see. Captain Payne would have been outside of the parade proper, you understand. Along with Sergeant-Major McInnes, he would have marched at various places looking for faults in the column. I was up front with my other officers and so I would not have been aware of Captain Payne's activities. He was to enter the Kirk after the other officers to see that the Colours were laid up in the front of the altar and so he would have gone down a side aisle. At the conclusion of the Parade, he would have marched back to the castle with the rest of us. I'm sorry, but that's about the best that I can tell you." The Colonel stood up and came around to where McNab was sitting. "You will try and keep this dreadful news about the Captain's murder out of the press? It would not be good for the Battalion, although I don't think that the troops will shed many tears."

"Is it possible to interview Sergeant-Major McInnes, Colonel?" McNab asked. The Colonel reached over to his telephone and instructed the orderly to fetch the

RSM from the Sergeants' Mess in the New Barracks which was next door and to have him meet the detective in the Visitors Waiting Room. McNab got up and shaking the Colonel's hand thanked him for his cooperation. He went down the stone steps of the Governor's House and followed the directions which the orderly had given him to the New Barracks which were nearby.

The New Barracks, the temporary home of the Eighth Battalion (Reserves), was a larger and more imposing stone building than the Governor's House. Only three floors appeared at the entrance level; the other three floors being below that and all six floors faced outwards with a view across the western part of the city. McNab entered the small side door which was set into the wall behind the two imposing windows which faced the small carpark which was now lined with vehicles. Inside, he found a tall, upright figure dressed in the Parade Uniform of a Regimental Sergeant Major. McNab went up to him and extended his hand:

"Sergeant-Major McInnes, I presume?" he asked. The big man did not smile but took McNab's hand in a crushing grip:

"Ay, A'm Sergeant-Major Mcinnes. Yer'e the detective, A'm thinkin. Come ower here tae the chairs an speir me yer questions. It's aboot our adutant, A believe?"

McNab followed the tall soldier over to a cluster of chairs set in front of the big windows near the building's entrance and sat down.

"Yes, that's right Sar' major. Can you tell me about Captain Payne's movements during and after the Church Parade?"

The Sergeant-Major straightened his kilt and looked hard at the detective. "Ye will ken thon A haed more importan' thangs tae dae. Lookin' after the sodiers as it were. A did, however notice thon the Adjutant wis doin his job at the back o the column as he shoud. Whan aw o the troops were fallen oot intae the Kirk, the captain followit an went intae side door tae help oot wi the ceremony. A did no see him on the march back an sae A assumed thon he went back wi the other officers."

McNab carefully wrote down the details into his small notebook and then looked up at the RSM. "What can you say about the relationship between Captain Payne and the other troops?" he asked.

The RSM waited awhile, and looked out of the windows before looking back directly at the detective. "A canna speak ill o the dead, mind, but Captain Payne wis no well likit bi onyone. He seemit tae resent bein wi the Battalion an haed some trubles on his mind. But havin says thon, A am sorry tae hear o his death."

"Is it possible to talk to those soldiers who were not occupied by being in the parade. They may have seen something of the late captain."

"Ay." The RSM said, slowly stroking his chin. "A think tha can be arrangit. It wad only be the twa piquets on duty at the castle an the duty men wha were fallen oot juist before the service startit, mind. They may have seen Captain Payne. Excuse me for a while. A'll see gin they are i the Soldiers' Mess."

The RSM stood up and walked back down the corridor. McNab wondered how many men he would have to interview. The answer came in a few minutes with the return of the RSM who was followed by four soldiers, still dressed in their Parade uniforms. The RSM continued:" Gin ye like, detective, A will tak the men ootside an ye can interview thaim separately in turn here. But A must insist thon A be present tae preven any impropriety, ye understand?"

McNab thought that such an informal interview would probably achieve more than taking these men down to the station, so he agreed to the RSM's proposal. Subsequently the soldiers were ushered outside where they sat on the small stone wall which ran next to the entrance.

The first two soldiers who McNab interviewed had been on Guard Duty in the small sentry boxes in front of the Gatehouse at the main entrance to the castle. They had been there for the entire length of the Church Parade and had watched as the Battalion had marched back into the castle. They had only been relieved after an additional hour. Both soldiers did not recall seeing Captain Payne march in with the other officers, but then their duty was to watch the Esplanade and its large crowd of spectators beyond the temporary barriers and not the marching column.

The next two soldiers had been the two Duty Men who were fallen out after the unit had assembled in their ranks in front of the Kirk. They had the responsibility of preceding the rest of the unit into the kirk and preparing the place where the Colours would be laid up for their blessing. Then they were to generally assist the participating ministers and their staff with the arrangements before the service. They also said that they had not seen Captain Payne for the entire time before the service and had joined the rank and file in the side pews when the unit had entered in to be seated.

McNab and meticulously taken down these statements and thanked the soldiers for their time and the interruption in their post-parade celebration. The RSM quietly dismissed the soldiers who went back along the corridor chattering about the interview. McNab thanked the RSM and left the barracks. The case was becoming more complex.

He continued to walk up the pathway and through the small archway of Foog's gate which led to the Upper Ward of the castle and to the Half Moon Battery. Here he found that the zealous uniformed officers had cordoned off the small elongated, curved battery with its nine 18-pounder cannons pointing outwards through their narrow embrasures. He remembered from somewhere in his reading that the Half Moon

Battery had been built on and around the ruins of the old medieval David's Tower which had been destroyed during a siege in the sixteenth century. The current cannons had been placed there during the Napoleonic Wars and the Battery was once the site for the popular One O'clock signal gun until it was moved to its present location on Mill's Mount Battery. He wondered what he would now find there.

4.

The snow was again falling lightly, it gave the view across to the university and Arthur's Seat beyond, a cold, grey, dismal look. McNab lent on the stone parapet feeling like some melancholy figure out of a Shakespearian play. As if on a theatrical cue, the ghost of his friend and mentor, Dr. Joseph Bell slowly appeared beside him:

"A good day for a haunting, is it not detective?" the spirit said with a laugh. "You seem troubled!"

"Yes, Dr. Bell." McNab replied, pulling his coat tighter to his body. "I am stumped as to how the body of Captain Payne ended up at the base of these walls when the last time he was seen was when he was going into the kirk before the service. None of the other soldiers reported seeing the Adjutant after his entrance into the kirk; and then he shows up here!"

The spirit walked over to the battlements facing the Esplanade and the start of the Royal Mile which led down to the kirk. He left no footprints in the light coating of new snow. "They say that the castle was once connected to the palace of Holyroodhouse at the end of the Royal Mile by a secret tunnel."

McNab suddenly stood erect and walked over to where the spirit was gazing. "Yes! I have heard that story, about the lone piper boy who was sent down a tunnel here but never returned. His ghost is said to play a lament from these very walls on some stormy nights."

"Bosh! You don't want to believe in those old ghost stories!" the spirit said with a grimace on his white face. "Why, they were around when I was a young student at yon university. About the drunken soldiers who tried to fire the One O'clock gun late at midnight and the shock of its recoil opened up a hole in the stone. Then were supposed to shove a wee boy to play the pipes, or the drum as some others say, so that they could follow the sound down the Mile. And when the sound suddenly stopped, the bravest of the soldiers went in and found only a dead end and no trace of the wee piper. Why, the One O'clock gun hadnae been fired until many years later. A good story for the gullible."

McNab turned away from the parapet: "Oh well, it was just an idea."

"And a good one, laddie. However, the better legend is the one that I was just about to tell you; listen! It was said that there was truly a tunnel running between the castle here and yon palace of Holyroodhouse. Queen Mary was said to have used it for some assignations between the palace and her suitors here in the castle. Others suggested that the tunnel was part of the escape route between St Giles' Cathedral, the High Kirk where your soldiers went today on parade, and the castle. Back in the days of the Reformation, being a priest on the wrong side was a dangerous occupation and many a kirk, stately home or even castle had its priest hole where they could hide. However, a connection between yon kirk and where you found the body might be a wee bit difficult to find. But wait! I'll have a wee look for you." With that, the spirit dissolved into his blue wisp of smoke and disappeared down one of the many stormwater gratings set into the floor of the battery.

McNab went over and peered down through the small, rectangular grating which had been cemented into the stone cobbles of the Battery floor. Soon, there reappeared a luminous blue mist filling the space below the grating. McNab jumped back and the mist came up and resolved itself into the figure of his ghostly friend.

"Well, now! That was an interesting experience!" the spirit said with a broad smile on his face and dusting himself down. "Yes, below that wee grating is the small tunnel which you would expect to be there to carry the water away. But I noticed that the floor had been patched with poor bricks, so I went deeper and after a while I did find our tunnel. What an experience! The tunnel is not very wide but high and suitable for a body to walk down – or drag a body if that is also needed."

McNab could hardly believe what his friend had just said; a possible route for Captain Payne to come or be brought from the kirk to the castle. The spirit continued:

"The tunnel goes right under here." He said, extending his arms out in a line running from the direction of the Royal Mile and back into the body of the castle. "Now, let us find a suitable entrance nearby."

McNab looked around and noticed that there was a set of stone steps surrounded by a metal railing in the corner of the Battery; just above where the body had been found below. He had not thought of such a possibility when he first examined the Battery but now, he raced down the steps followed by the spirit who swiftly glided behind him. At the bottom of the stairwell was a stout wooden door with an ornate door ring and metal lock.

"This was possibly the Old Guard Room and Armoury when the original One O'clock gun was fired from this location," said the spirit.

McNab tugged and pushed at the old wooden door without success. "Can you unlock it from inside?" he said to the spirit who was closely examining the lock.

"Ah well, that could be a problem!" he replied. "Yon lock is an old one; nineteenth century perhaps." He gave a short laugh. "Well! That was also my generation! But let me try."

With that, the spirit dissolved into to his usual wisp of blue smoke which narrowed down and went into the large keyhole of the lock. Nothing happened for a while, then McNab heard some faint noises within the lock itself and then, with a loud click, the door swung open. Dr. Bell was leaning against the wall just inside the door wiping his brow with a handkerchief. "Indeed, that was a hard one! I had to cram myself into that wee lock housing and turn the mechanism myself. Not too easy, even for a spirit. But come in laddie and let's look at what is inside."

McNab entered the small room which had walls of the large blocks of stone which formed this part of Edinburgh Castle. It did not contain much; a large metal chest painted in a drab, khaki colour, a small chair and table and an old wooden wardrobe standing against the wall just inside the door. McNab could see no grand entrance to a tunnel nor anything else of importance, except the metal chest which he assumed had once contained the powder charges for the original 64-pounder gun. He pulled his mobile phone from his jacket pocket and switch on the 'light' app.

"What do you see now laddie with that wee light contraption?" the spirit said with a wry smile.

"Nothing much! There's not much to see" confessed McNab.

"Aye it's what is not here that is important. Look to the floor near yon wardrobe. Can you see what is missing?"

McNab shone the feeble light towards the old battered wardrobe and saw what Dr. Bell had seen. There was a patch of floor to the right of the wardrobe which was not as dusty as the rest of the floor. "Why, this wardrobe has been moved!" he exclaimed.

"Right, laddie! Now let us move it back to its original place and see what lies behind it."

McNab and Dr. Bell grasped the side of the wardrobe nearest the door and pushed. It was a heavy wardrobe and McNab felt that his ethereal companion could not possibly be adding much force. Eventually it was moved along the wall to where it had originally stood. McNab shone his light to the wall which had been hidden by the wardrobe. There was a small, arched doorway cut into the large blocks of stone, However, this had been bricked up by old bricks, most of which had been broken down to make a small opening about the size which would allow a person to enter. He carefully looked inside and found that the missing bricks had been neatly stacked inside of the cavity. Beyond, he could see that there was a set of steep steps going down in the direction of the old drain which the spirit had examined. "A tunnel!" he exclaimed.

The spirit looked at him a sighed." Aye and what did you expect? If you will permit me, I shall do a quick exploration of yon dark tunnel. Your little lantern would not do justice to the darkness and it could be dangerous down there. You might get hurt or even killed if this old tunnel collapses. On the other hand, I do not need the light and am already dead." He laughed."

Mc Nab saw the sense in Bell's statement and his little joke and so agreed to wait outside in the fresh air of the night.

"I will be back soon," promised the spirit who went into his luminous blue mist form and disappeared down the steep steps into the darkened tunnel.

McNab was used to his friend's ability to go anywhere without the usual time frame imposed on the living, but this time, there was a notable delay until the spirit rematerialized on the battlements of the Half Moon Battery. He looked very pleased with himself.

"We are in luck, my young friend!" he said smiling. "This is indeed that legendary tunnel which joins the castle to Holyroodhouse. However, it is totally blocked at some great distance along by a wall of bricks similar to those of our first arched doorway. But, not far back from this wall, I found another arched doorway with its bricks removed just like the one here.

Through it is another set of steep, stone steps leading upward; guess where they went?"

"Up into St, Giles' kirk I would guess." McNab said with a knowing look.

"Aye." Replied Bell. "Right up into a small room with a wooden wall on this side containing a hidden priest hole which opens out into a basement room of the kirk."

"Then we have our route from the kirk to the castle along which our Captain Payne could have come - voluntarily or not."

"Exactly!" said the spirit. "You find the one who has the key to this door and you have your murderer. That is the key to your problem. Ha, ha!"

McNab was happy. This discovery explained how Captain Payne had got from the Kirk to the castle. It was reasonable, he thought that Payne was probably killed in the kirk and his body dragged through the tunnel. It seemed unlikely that Captain Payne had come through the tunnel of his own free will or even under duress and then been killed here on the battlements. Either way, his body had then been thrown over the wall to make it look like suicide.

"I suppose that my next step would be to go to St. Giles and examine the room in the basement for any signs of a struggle." McNab said, looking at the spirit with an uncertain look.

"Aye. That'll be the logical thing to do, laddie. You'll find that the priest hole as a slightly protruding panel in the wooden wall and it slides to the left. The spirit said before smiling and slowly disappearing.

5.

The next day, luckily was a Monday, the snow had stopped falling and the sun now shone with its golden light a sparkling glitter on the white crust on the rooves and streets of the city. In some places, long blue-white icicles hung down from the railings and some of the exposed gutters. He felt elated that he and his ghostly friend had discovered the possible site of the murder of Captain Payne and how his body had arrived at the castle. He had telephoned the secretary at the cathedral and as it wasn't a long distance between there and his station, he had decided to walk. He whistled in the cold air as he walked along the footpath across North Bridge Road which passed over the railway lines and into the Old Town. He had timed his morning walk so that he could arrive at St. Giles' by nine when it would be open. It would be a convenient time when he could interview the incumbent minister and his staff and then search the lower basement for the room containing the hidden priest hole.

At the cathedral, he walked up the few steps at its entrance and under its imposing archway. He was met just inside by an austere-looking older man who introduced himself as Mr. McAlistair, the Head Beadle of the High Kirk.

"Och, now! Yu wad be the detective Mr. McNab. I assume?" he said in a Highland lilt." Ye have been expectit. Come inside. Hou can I help ye?"

McNab took the proffered hand and followed the Beadle inside where he explained the nature of his visit and the desire to examine the basement rooms of the cathedral. The entrance to this august building, once the Catholic cathedral of the city before the Reformation, faced towards the castle. It would be probable McNab thought, that the entrance to his basement room should be not far from this entrance. He was wrong. After some definitive questions from the austere McAlistair, McNab was led halfway down the Nave and then into a side chapel. Here, they went across in front of the pulpit and into another small space which was decorated with many plaques of famous writers, including that of Robert Louis Stevenson. This room McAlistair called the Moray Aisle and in one far corner, hidden by a small railing was a flight of stone steps going down to the basement of the kirk. These steps opened out into another small room which contained many small shelves and cupboards on a bare stone floor. On the far side of the room was a wooden wall made up of several, small rectangular panels. McNab noticed this as he turned to the Beadle and asked if he may be left alone to examine the room.

"Oh ay! But I'll be juist upstairs gin ye neit me. Dae no touch anything, do ye ken?"

McNab thanked him and took out a more substantial flashlight than his phone ap and began to look around. Suddenly a side panel of the wooden wall opened and Dr. Bell in a more opaque mode crawled through.

"What a small hole this would be for a priest!" he uttered as he stood up "but I thought that I try it and enter in a more traditional manner than simply passing through the wall. I hope that you appreciated that!" he said with a laugh.

"Thanks!" McNab replied continuing with his detailed search. The light moving across the last stone step showed a darker stain on the edge of the lowest stone steps. He bent over and examined it more closely.

"What have you found, my young friend?" Bell asked, coming across the room to peer over McNab's shoulder.

"I could be wrong, but there is a darker stain here on the edge of this grey stone step. It could be dried blood."

Bell knelt down and looked at the stain which McNab illuminated more closely, shining the flashlight beam at an angle for better reflection.

"Ay, that it looks like." Said Bell with some confidence. "You'll notice how it shines more than the dull grey of the rest of the stone step."

McNab reached into his coat pocket and pulled out a small plastic bag. From his trouser pocket he took out his small pocket knife and scraped off some of the stain into the bag. The colour of the fragments was reddish-brown; consistent with that of dried blood.

"I will get the Forensic boys to do some DNA tests on this and see if it belongs to our victim." McNab said "but I am almost positive that this is where our poor adjutant was killed."

"And who do you think would have done the killing?" the spirit asked with a gleam in his eyes."

McNab looked up and said: "I would think that it was someone attached to the parade this morning rather than any of the staff here in the kirk. Our most likely suspects are the two Duty Men who would have been here in the kirk with Captain Payne during the Church Service."

"Bravo! You are now starting to come up with some good theories from your deductions, detective. That's the spirit; and I should know about that!" Bell said with his usual dry sense of humour. "You now have all of the clues, so I'll leave you to go and collect your suspects. Goodbye for now," and with that, Bell disappeared leaving McNab to go back up the stairs to the old Beadle.

Late that afternoon, having secured a Search Warrant, McNab went back to the barracks at Edinburgh Castle with two uniformed Constables and arrested the two former Duty Men, Corporal Jock McTavish and Private Jamie Fergusson. A subsequent search of their lockers soon produced a large, antique key which

McNab carefully put into an evidence bag with his handkerchief so as not to smudge any fingerprints on it.

Back at the station, McNab was ready to interview each man in turn. His friend, Detective Sergeant Olivia Kerr, who had just returned from her assignment in Glasgow, came over and suggested that he interview Private Fergusson first of all:

"The youngest pig always squeals the loudest." She advised with a wink of a beautiful eye and this is what McNab did. At first, the young soldier said nothing; he was obviously scared and shaken but said nothing. It was not until McNab reminded him that he was under suspicion of murder. That the young soldier broke down a flood of tears and gave his account of the demise of Captain Payne and a garbled plea of innocence:

"Oh God help me! It wis no murder, it wis an accident! The stoopid idjit pokit Jock wi his little stick, sae Jock hit him one an he went doun. E hit his heed on tha step. It wis no murder. An thon's the truth o't!"

The second suspect was a harder man to crack but when told that his friend had confessed and described how the Adjutant had been killed, he gave up with a sigh and told McNab the entire story.

It seems that McTavish had long ago heard about the legend of the ghostly piper from his grandfather who had sworn that the story was true because he had seen it himself. Grandfather McTavish had said that as a young man, he was on a work team repairing the old drains on the Half Moon Battery. Digging into its old stone work, they had accidently pushed a crowbar through into a cavity below the old brick drain. The crowbar had gone through the roof of a long tunnel which ran parallel to the Royal Mile. Afraid of being blamed for further damage, they had quickly bricked up the cavity and finished their work.

Much later, when the young McTavish had grown up, joined the Army and was posted to the castle for his Annual Continuous Training, he had gone with his young friend Jamie Fergusson to look for his grandfather's tunnel. They had chosen the night when they had volunteered for a late roving piquet and had gone directly to the Battery. Here they had found the set of steps which had led down to the old wooden door. Now, McTavish in his civilian occupation was a locksmith by trade, so the next day, he arranged for his sister to bring up to the castle his set of keys appropriate to that type of lock.

Having found one which would open the door, the same key found hidden in his locker, he and Fergusson had gone back the next night with a flashlight and searched the room. They eventually found it bricked up behind an old wardrobe which they then pushed aside. They easily knocked out most of the ancient bricks, which they stacked inside the tunnel, and then went down the long, steep stone steps into the tunnel itself. They explored it for some length until they found that it had been blocked up by more brickwork so they retraced their steps and explored a side alcove and steps which they found led up to the wooden panels of the priests' hole in the kirk.

As it was late at night, there was no one in the huge cathedral and they found a small side door with a modern latch from which they could go out into Parliament Square. This was convenient to them as it was just down from the Deacon Brody Tavern closer to the castle and a favourite drinking venue for the younger set. Now on a quiet night, free of duty, they could sneak in to the room on the battlements, change into civilian clothes and then go down the tunnel and to the tavern for a bender. Their work uniforms would be stored out of sight in the old wardrobe.

When pressed further on the murder of Captain Payne, McTavish also protested his innocence and gave an account of that fateful morning. He said that he and Fergusson had volunteered to be the Duty Men at the Church Parade so that their secret exit was not uncovered by any of their suspicious colleagues who must have had an inkling of their nightly visits to the tavern. Having provide some assistance before the service started, they had been asked by the Beadle to bring up some other necessary items from the storeroom. Here they had also found where the flagons of sacramental wine were kept and decided to help themselves to a 'wee dram' before returning to the service. Unfortunately, they had been caught by Captain Payne who had come down to find the two men whom he suspected of malingering. He had angrily abused both men and had emphasised his displeasure by poking McTavish, a corporal, with his swagger stick. As an instinctive reaction, the soldier had lashed out and struck his officer on his chin and he had fallen backwards, striking his head on the sharp edge of the stone step, killing him instantly. In a panic, the two soldiers had quickly dragged the body down through the tunnel and out onto the battlements of the castle. With no one in sight, they had thrown it over the parapet in the hope that it would be believed that the unhappy adjutant had committed suicide.

They then hurried back and re-joined their comrades in the kirk and had marched back with them to their barracks in the castle after the long service.

The next evening McNab was well-satisfied with himself. The case had been solved and more accolades had been given to him by his colleagues back at the station. He walked back to the Old Town and up to the Cathedral; his curiosity had got the better of him and there was something that McTavish had said in his confession which had sparked his curiosity.

There was a late-night service in the Cathedral and McNab quietly entered and quickly went down the far aisle and into the darkened side chapel without being noticed. He went down the steps and into the small basement room where he turned on his small flashlight and found the secret panel of the priest hole. Going through it and down the old stone steps, he turned to the right at its foot rather than left which led back to the castle. He searched the old tunnel and its old stonework until he came to a small arched doorway similar to the one which he and Bell had found back at the castle. This doorway too, had been bricked up with the old coarse bricks. He examined it more closely and found that at its top, several layers of bricks did not appear to have mortar between them. He reached up and grabbed the edge of one of the higher bricks and found that it moved. The bricks had been moved a long time ago but then loosely replaced. Had this been where the tune of the lone boy piper had stopped? Had he been able to remove these bricks, scamper through and then carefully replaced them so that no one would find his exit route from the army and his escape from his tormentors? McNab smiled and thought that this would be a fitting end to this legend and that somewhere, the young lone piper had at last found some peace.

Time had passed quickly for McNab in the tunnel and so it was late when he quietly climbed back up to the main nave of the kirk which was now in darkness. He was able to find the side door which McTavish had described. It had a relatively modern lock, so he was able to lock it behind him as he went out into the cold air of the city. It was snowing lightly again, as it did on the first day of the case, and as he walked back through the gloom of the night towards the castle and a storm brewing to the east, he heard the eery tune of a lament being piped from the castle's battlements.

The Dragon's Tooth

Hamish McNab was happy; very happy. He was walking hand in hand with his beautiful colleague, Detective Sergeant Olivia Kerr through a lovely field of heather. The early morning summer sun was sparkling off these little pink flowers as far as the eye could see. He was happy. Then he was rudely awoken by the sharp call of his mobile phone right next to his ear. Switching on the bedside lamp, he looked at the time through sleep-bleary eyes; one-thirty-six on a cold Edinburgh morning.

"Hello?" he said, trying to come awake and a little annoyed at the time of the call.

"McNab!" came an even more annoyed voice of his superior, Detective Chief Inspector MacFarlane; a man not noted for his compassion. "McNab, there's been a kerfuffle over at the National Museum. A rather garbled call came through to the station reporting that someone has been attacked by a dragon. You're the one with the science degree, so you can talk to the boffins better than I."

McNab poked his ear thinking that he had misheard: "A dragon?"

"Aye, that's what I said; a bloody dragon!"

"Argh, Chief! I think that somebody's winding us up!"

"I'm nae a bampot! The call came in from the Nightwatchman, old Willie Swayne. The Duty Sergeant knew him as his sergeant when he was a Constable. Now get yoursel' over there! I'm sending a car fer ya!" Click!

"Yes, sir!" McNab said into the unheeding phone and looked around on the floor for his clothes. Quickly dressing, he quietly let himself out of the small room which he rented in Mrs. McElroy's boarding house and down the stairs to the cold, darkened street. It wasn't long before a car glided quietly up to the kerb;

Mrs. McElroy had long preferred police officers as her boarders but could not abide their noisy, late night comings-and-goings. McNab jumped in and closed the door softly.

"Whit is up, sir. It's a wee bit earla fur detective work? isnae it?" the officer in the front passenger seat said, turning to look quizzically at McNab.

"That it is Jamie." McNab replied. He knew both officers well as he had only recently been promoted out of the Uniform Branch. Jamie McNulty was a Senior Constable and a reliable hand when it came to some of the rough stuff encountered by the police. His driver, Constable Kyle Murdock was also another good man and was rapidly learning the ways of his older partner. "Some nonsense about a dragon, so this should be an interesting call." Both officers looked at each other but got back to driving through the narrow streets which led up to the buildings of the National Museum of Scotland.

The car pulled up in Chalmers Street outside of the Victorian Venetian Renaissance facade of the old Royal Scottish Museum. This had been the original museum before it combined with the adjacent and more modern construction of the Museum of Scotland to become the National Museum of Scotland.

McNab and the two constables left the car and walked smartly up the wide flight of steps to the centre of the three doors of the entrance, which they had noticed was slightly ajar. Inside, they found the old Nightwatchman sitting on a chair visibly shaken.

McNab went up to the old man who raised a white frightened face to the detective:

"Och, thenk God 'at ye hae arrived! Ah am a micht shaken. Tha body's in thaur. in th' Gran' Gallry, but tak' caur min'. It's Reit under th' dragon."

McNab turned to the younger constable: "Go with Mr. Swayne and get him a cup of tea; he looks like he could do with one."

"Och a wee dram woods be mair loch it, cheil," replied the old man as the constable helped him up.

McNab directed the Senior Constable to remain at the front door whilst he went through the vestibule into the darkened expanse of the grand gallery. This is the huge central hall of cast iron construction that rises the full four stories of the building before being capped with a long, extended glass cupola. There was only a small security light at the far end and the torch which McNab shone around the long gallery made moving shadows which played on his imagination. As a small boy, his parents had often taken him to the old Royal Scottish Museum and once, a guide with a warped sense of humour had told the young McNab that sometimes at night, the animals all come alive to wander through the building.

It was with this unreasonable childish apprehension that he found old Mr. Swayne's dragon.

At the far end of the long gallery was a dramatically reconstructed skeleton of a *Tyrannosaurus rex.* It's moving shadow on the side wall certainly gave it some semblance of active aggression. Just below its impressive head and long jaws was a body of a man.

The body lay in crumpled heap, stretched over the metal railing, its two arms outstretched as if appealing for help. It lay on its back and there were many deep puncture marks around its chest through the white high collared coat which the victim wore. McNab looked up at the huge head of the dinosaur immediately above the body; its long, curved teeth shining in the torch light.

2.

McNab shone the torchlight at the body again and then back up at the jaws of the dinosaur above him. No! Not possible, his scientific training told him, but there was still some trace of the fey of his ancient Celtic ancestors which gave him some concern.

He looked around at the immense space and could see nothing else which was at all suspicious; just the crumpled body below those fearsome jaws. He sat down on the railing next to the body. What would Dr. Bell think of this; his mind was surely more rooted in science and natural causes than his?

Almost as if on cue, the thin wisp of blue smoke with which McNab had become familiar, suddenly resolved into the more solid figure of his ghostly friend.

"Ah! My young friend. You seem to need my help once more. Don't be alarmed at this familiarity; I am merely interested in your development of a deductive detective and of the interesting situations in which you find yourself. Besides, it gets rather boring simply going to my old haunts and floating about remembering old times."

McNab gave the spirit a weak grin and looked up apologetically: "Do you think that this beast had anything to do with this murder?" he asked.

"Oh, undoubtably!" replied the spirit. "otherwise, the body would not be here. But as to it causing the poor man's death, I would most certainly think not. But let us examine the body to be certain."

Bell glided over to the body and peered down closely to its chest then looked up at the teeth of the dinosaur. "Most interesting! See over yonder at that desk. There is a container holding some long pencils in it. Be a good fellow and retrieve one for me."

McNab went over to the small counter where there was a small container of pencils and a tray of student worksheets for young visitors. He took the longest one out and walked back to where Bell was standing next to the body.

"Now, Detective McNab! Kindly examine several of the largest wounds on the victim's chest by placing your instrument into them. Please be thorough and test both the depth and width of each wound."

McNab bent down and poked the pencil deep into several of the wounds. He found that the main wounds were consistently about twenty centimetres in length and wider at their tops going down to a point at base. He described his findings to Dr. Bell who again looked up at the dinosaur's mouth.

"Most interesting indeed! The description of those wounds would be consistent with the shape and length of the teeth of our bony friend here, but I think that their use in this murder was most unlikely. But what can you also tell me about those wounds?"

McNab went closer to the body and looked at each wound: "Well, there does not seem to be the amount of blood from the wounds as one would expect; especially if our Tyrannosaurus did the deed."

"Precisely! Now look at the victim's face and tell me what is unusual. I am sure that your past experience with cadavers at the Old Medical School would give you some experience here."

McNab looked away from the wounds which dotted the victim's chest and up to its face. It was the face of a relatively young man; the skin now was white and the pupils of the eyes had long since clouded over but the whites were covered in small, red spots of blood. The lank hair was a pale blonde colour and its lips were a light blue. There also seemed to be some slight bruising around the base of the neck. The young detective described his observations to the sprit who stood back with his arms folded and a look of satisfaction on his white face.

"Perfect! So, then my diligent student, what can you deduce?" he said.

McNab was uncertain at first but then summoned up some courage and made his hypothesis:

"Well, I think that our victim may have been strangled by another person, then taken out here and then stabbed with some implement which would be similar to the teeth of the Tyrannosaurus. Considering the rigid state of the body, I would say that there were quite a few hours between the suffocation and the stabbing. The lack of any large amount of blood on the body would suggest that the wounds were inflicted on a dead body which had already achieved a certain amount of rigor mortis. This is also suggested by the rigidity of the arms which were probably used to drag the body to be dumped here."

"Capital! capital!" exclaimed Bell, much pleased with his student's hypothesis. "You see the marks on the neck are only small and somewhat faded suggesting that if he were strangled, it was some time ago. However, the red spots on the whites of his eyes are most certainly signs of strangulation. They are referred to by us medical types as 'petechiae' and they can last for some time. Go on, man! What else?"

McNab looked around the floor which had not yet been cleaned and there were scuff marks everywhere. However, he could add more to his story: "Well, the floor shows the previous day's wear and tear and judging by the rather short, rotund figure of the deceased, I would say that he would not have been dragged very far; perhaps from one of the offices which appear to be on this floor. Carrying such a dead weight, literally, from an upper story would have been difficult."

Bell clapped his hands together in joy:" Yes, exactly my conclusion. The man was probably killed sometime late yesterday in some non-public area then, very much later, dragged out here and dumped in front of this beastie. The reason for that, however, escapes me. Some questions will need to be answered and so for the moment, I will leave you to your case. Goodbye." With that, Bell slowly disappeared into the darkness of the museum.

McNab found Kyle Murdock and old Willie Swayne, the Nightwatchman sitting in the small room shared by him and his colleagues. It was a very small room with just a tiny wooden table and two chairs; all of which could have easily been exhibited in another part of the museum. There was a small bench with a sink and a gas ring which the young constable had lit and the old man was now clutching a hot cup of very strong black tea. The constable jumped up as McNab entered and McNab gave him a little nod suggesting that he should wait outside. McNab sat down on the chair and lightly patted the old man on his knee.

"Well, Mr. Swayne. Are you up to answering a few questions?" he said gently. The old man held on to his cup with both hands as it was cold in this little room.

"Och aye. Ah can dae 'at fur ye, laddie" he said, a slight tremble in his voice showed that he was still in shock.

"Nothing hard, Mr. Swayne and I will be brief. Tell me about your duty last night and finding the body, please."

"Aye, weel, there's nae much tae teel. Ah took ower frae wee Angus Bruce at th' usual time; that'll be at fifteen minutes tae twal. He hud naethin' tae report an' sae he went haem."

"And when did you find the body, Mr. Swayne?"

"Ah noo, 'at was a shock it was an' aw. Th' dragon, ur whit th' wee boffins caa a tyrano-what's-m- caa-it is at th' far end ay th' Gran' Hall. Sae Ah did nae see th' body until Ah hud inspected th' upper galleries. When Ah cam doon - weel thaur it was! Aw haverin' under them lang teeth. Ah tint it, ye kin an' ran tae th' fron' desk an' called ye fellows."

"Do you remember at what time you found the body?"

"Weel, nae exactly, but mah times ur bonnie reular min'. We aw hae uir sit ways ay gonnae aboot the museum. It woods hae taken me abit an hoor tae swatch intae aw ay th' upper galleries afair comin' doon haur; say abit a wee efter a won in th' mornin'. Ah rang th' polis straecht efter."

"Did you notice anything else that might have been out of place?"

"Och no! Won body's enaw fur th' nicht. Aw was guid upstairs an' Ah did ninae sae much aroond efter findin' th' body."

"Lastly, when do the cleaners come in to clean the floor?"

The old man looked around as if to have noticed the floor for the first time: "Aye. It's a micht ontidy noo but they come in earl' in th' morn abit six".

McNab thanked the old man and called Constable Murdock in and asked him to take the old man home. Outside, Senior Constable Jamie McNulty had cordoned off the main entrance with the usual masses of 'Police' tape, he had also found a sign stating that the museum was closed. This he put out at the top of the stone steps just before the entrance.

The Forensic Team had arrived much later, grumbling about the early morning hour and complaining that murders should happen only in business hours. This was usual for them, McNab thought, as they were very much experienced at being called out at all hours in all weathers to many extreme locations. Finn McMurray, the senior of the two-man team had looked at the body, then up at the head of the dinosaur and then at McNab. He raised an eyebrow and gave a wry grin:

"Now dinnae tell me, Hamish, but this man wis eaten bi our wee beastie here?"

"Sorry, Finn. I think that your tests will find that he has been strangled many hours ago and dragged here after he became stiff. The wounds were inflicted into the body well after death and so there's not much blood"

Tom Graham, the second member of the team looked at McNab with mock disappointment and said in his nasal English voice: "What a pity, old chap. Here I was hoping for something really exciting. 'Death by Tyrannosaurus' would have been a very interesting report to make."

It would have been about seven in the morning when the first member of the museum staff arrived. This was Dr. Edward Brown, the Director who had been advised of the murder as soon as the station had thought appropriate. Naturally he was shocked at the murder but he had summoned up his courage and identified the body as Dr. Frederick McKenzie, the Assistant Head of the Natural Sciences Department.

Dr. Brown took McNab into the Staff Common Room, a rather large room which also acted as a venue for meetings. He sat down at the long, central table with the detective and gave a detailed statement about the museum, his own affairs and that of the late Dr. McKenzie. McNab took all of this down in his notebook, looking for a possible motive for the crime.

"Dr. McKenzie had an international reputation as a vertebrate palaeontologist," the Director stated. "Well-known for his papers on the megafauna of the Late Cretaceous. The acquisition of our large *Tyrannosaurus* specimen here, albeit on temporary loan from the Canadians, was considered by Dr. McKenzie as being a prize achievement for the museum- and for himself, of course."

"Can you think of anyone who would want to kill Dr. McKenzie?" McNab asked.

"Well, no! Not really." Dr Brown answered. "McKenzie could get on one's nerves occasionally; he lived and breathed his work on sauropods and had little patience for those other mere mortals who did not."

McNab was interested in the personality of the deceased so he asked the Director to elaborate further. Dr. Brown explained that McKenzie was generally considered inoffensive for most of the time and was sometimes called 'Chubbysaurus' behind his back because of his fixation with his work and his short, fat stature. He could occasionally show his intolerance towards the technical staff who were slow to follow his demands in setting up the displays or with members of the financial section when it came to allocation of museum funds. Around the other academics, he generally kept himself at a distance preferring quiet indifference to friendship. There was nothing in his manner nor with his work which would have led to his violent death. As to the location of the body below the jaws of the *Tyrannosaurus* skeleton, Dr. Brown could only suggest that it was possibly an obscure reference to McKenzie's fixation which was well-known to all who worked at the museum and who had to tolerate his continual discourses on the superior nature of vertebrate palaeontology.

Bell noted this all down and, apart from some agreement with the Director as to the dumping of the body below 'Scotty', the *Tyrannosaurus*, he could not find anything in this description of a slightly obsessed academic to provide a motive for his murder.

When asked why he had referred to the dinosaur skeleton as 'Scotty', the Director had laughed and explained that the actual fossil was discovered in 1991 in Eastend, Saskatchewan, Canada and to christen it, the excavators had used the only bottle available, a bottle of good Scotch whiskey, hence the nickname. This skeleton, which was only on loan during a worldwide tour, is only a very good replica made from steel and resin; the original lithified bones are too fragile for full skeletal construction were still back in Canada under storage. McNab was glad of having two years of geology in his degree but could now understand why his chief hated talking to scientists – 'boffins' in his terminology.

It was going to be a long day. One by one the staff at the museum arrived, mostly after eight prior to the museum's opening at ten. Naturally most seemed shocked upon hearing of the murder. Each in turn was taken to the common room by a member of the uniform branch. McMurray had called the station and had seen to the removal of the body, so there was really nothing to show of the grisly scene except a slightly bent railing below the dinosaur's jaws. The Director had gathered all of the staff into the large common room and had called in 'wee' Angus Bruce, the other Nightwatchman who was well over six feet tall. Dr. Brown then personally introduced his Executive Staff who were directors or heads of departments involved in the sub-divisions of types of exhibits, finances and administration.

Once everyone had settled into a chair or had found a convenient place around the wall, McNab asked each person to identify themselves, to give their job descriptions and their whereabouts during the previous day. Most had come to the museum as usual and had began the day's normal routine. The financial staff were mainly cloistered into their cramped office space and had left promptly just after five in the afternoon; the museum's closing time. The technical staff had had an easy day with little maintenance and few exhibits to set up or repair and so had little reason to stay after closing time. The administration staff likewise had little to offer, as their main contacts were those of the executive staff or the general public so had little contact with the technical nor academic staff. It seemed that only the academic staff involved with the scientific or cultural sides of the exhibits had much to do with the late Frederick McKenzie.

Nightwatchman Bruce had briefly outlined his duties stating that he had arrived a little before four in the afternoon to start his four-to-midnight shift when he handed over to Willie Swayne. Part of his responsibility was to ensure that the museum was clear of visitors before closing time and to let any late staff members out before locking the entrance doors and switching off the lights. He was certain that only Dr. McKenzie had stayed back later after closing time; something which he was sometimes in the habit of doing. He also produced the Attendance Book which was always kept here in the common room for staff to log in when they started work in the morning and to log out before they left. McNab looked down the column for yesterday's attendance and found only the signature of Dr. McKenzie absent from the long list of names.

Content with these statements, McNab asked the Nightwatchman:

"Other than yourself, who would have the key to enter the museum at night?"

The tall Nightwatchman answered in a slow drawl:" Tha' wad only be the directors an the academic staff, sir. They often neit tae come i at odd hours whan special events occur an sae they have a key tae the side door oot on West College Street."

McNab continued: "And did you see anyone after the doors were closed yesterday?"

Bruce stroked his chin and looked up at the ceiling: "Na, only Dr. Mckenzie wha wis workin back late again; thaur was still a lecht under his duir when Ah checked th' main hall aboot six. A clearit oot the museum o visitors well before five an sae A wis at the main door at tha' time tae lock it up. A recollect seein most o the staff leave. Dr. Svoboda wis the last oot an he says guid nicht tae me an askit me tae lock up."

"How long did Dr. McKenzie work for that night?" McNab asked.

"Och, nae long a tal. Perhaps an hoor or sae, A wad guess. Ye see, A startit on ma rounds an whan A returnit at aboot seven, his door wis closit an thare wis na licht under it."

McNab thanked the tall nightwatchman and then went into a small office nearby which he found was, in fact, that of the late Assistant Director McKenzie. He had asked one of the newly-arrived uniform constables to show each member of staff into the room in the order of technical, financial and administrative staff; leaving the academics and executives until last. Each member of staff was interviewed and McNab wrote down their statements; these he would review back at the station. It was late in the afternoon and darkness was beginning to creep into the old building when he finally finished the interviews and he had allowed all of the staff to go home. Tonight, the museum would be considered a 'crime scene' and several of the uniform officers were detailed to search the buildings and check that all of the doors and windows had been locked. He also had taken the precaution of obtaining the keys to the side door possessed by the senior staff.

Whilst the officers were searching the extremities of the vast museum, McNab went out and found Dr. McKenzie's office; a small room just off the main hall. There was no sign of blood nor a scuffle here, indeed, he had the impression that the room had been meticulously cleaned and ordered. Even though it had been stated by Director Brown that Dr. McKenzie was obsessed with detail, such a tidy room did not fit into McNab's experience nor picture of an academic's study.

He was casually looking at the many exhibits which the good doctor kept in several glass-topped cases at the far end of the room when he heard a familiar voice at his side.

"Regard that long tooth in the central cabinet, laddie. What can you see?"

McNab turned to find the solid form of Dr. Bell looking over his shoulder. The young detective smiled, grateful that his friend had returned. He looked back at the central glass-topped cabinet and peered carefully at the long, curved tooth on display. It was about forty centimetres long and curved down from a relatively broad base to a sharp point. It was a deep brown colour with a narrow channel running down its length from the centre of its base to the point.

"It seems a remarkable cutting tooth, the shape and the channel running down it suggests that it would rip into flesh nicely. It seems rather smooth and clean for a fossil"

"Aye, that it would," replied Bell but don't look at the tooth, look at its surroundings."

McNab looked at the white paper below the tooth and the neat, computer-written label below it. There was a distinct discolouration of the underlying paper at one corner of the label and along the edge of the tooth. "Why! It looks like the specimen has been recently moved! The paper below these specimens has been slightly discoloured by sunlight but not at that corner edge. The other specimens in this and the other cases do not appear to have been moved for some time and so the paper underneath is of a uniform shade."

"Excellent, McNab. Now stand back and look at the cases themselves. What do you notice about the central case?"

McNab had missed the obvious; the central case containing the tooth lacked the small padlock which were on the locks of the other cases.

Bell continued: "So then, detective. What can you deduce from all of that?"

McNab looked up at his friend with understanding in his eyes. "It looks like that tooth has been taken out of this case recently then put back in a hurry. Whoever did this did not have time to put the padlock back on but was probably more occupied with other matters."

"Like getting away from the scene of a murder!" Bell suggested, "But that would be a very weak hypothesis, you understand."

McNab looked around the room for the small padlock and found it on the floor not far from the cases. "Possibly, but I also think that a man like Dr. McKenzie, noted for his attention to detail, would have taken the tooth out then pit it back in its exact position then replaced the padlock. It was possibly someone else who removed then replaced the tooth. Let's look at the label."

McNab and Bell looked closely at the neatly-typed label which read '_Tyrannosaurus rex_ [probable only] – Late Cretaceous Wyoming'.

"'Tyrant King Lizard' if my Latin is still intact!" said Bell with some satisfaction. I am not familiar with the taxonomy of geological specimens but this seems to be a real tooth of yonder beastie. What do you think?"

"Well, Dr. Bell, my vertebrate palaeontology is rather limited but this tooth looks real and not a replica like in the jaws of the skeleton outside. I vaguely recall that T-rex teeth were usually not greater than thirty centimetres long."

"Now, I'm not a betting man mind," Bell laughed, "but I would wager that the shape and size of yon tooth would match the wounds in the corpse of the late academic."

McNab carefully took the tooth out of the case using his handkerchief and placed it into a plastic bag which he had in his pocket. He also made a mental note to get a pair of surgical gloves when he next returned to the station.

Hearing the footsteps of the returning constables, Bell gave McNab a cheery wave and disappeared.

3

The next morning, Hamish McNab, Detective Constable, sat at his cluttered desk in the dingy corner of the big room in the unattractive complex of Police buildings in Fettes Avenue. His desk had become even more cluttered with the many pieces of paper which he had torn out of his big notebook. These were the statements he had taken down from the staff back at the National Museum of Scotland. He really was an orderly person; his science studies had seen to that, but he did have a problem of uncertainty and how to order these statements. Eventually he had cleared his desk of all of the other old reports, log books and other paraphernalia and had catalogued them according to the staffing categories back at the museum: administrative; financial; technical; and academic.

He read through each report in each of the four piles on his desk and then read them again. As far as access to the late Dr. McKenzie, none of the staff appeared to have stayed back at the museum with the recently deceased. Only the Nightwatchman, 'wee' Angus Bruce had been in the building around the time of the murder sometime just after closing time at five in the afternoon; except the murderer of course. He and his relieving colleague, Willie Swayne who had reported the murder after one the next morning had little or no motive for killing McKenzie.

Likewise, for the administrative, financial and technical staff. All of the personnel in these categories had little to do with the deceased and the Head of Finances, Fiona McIntosh had stated that there had not been any regularities in the finances of the university. Dr. McKenzie had always been economic in his use of funds but always was a 'wee bit annoying' in his many requests for more funding. Hardly a motive for murder. The technical staff generally were sometimes chastised by McKenzie if they were slow to set up his displays or carry out small technical duties, but in the main they had usually put these complaints aside as being typical of a finicky academic and so subject to being ignored. No motives here. Only the academic staff showed some interest as they were more involved in Dr. McKenzie's daily routine and work.

Dr, Brown, the museum's Director had given McNab a detailed rundown of McKenzie's work and personality as well as his view of the relationships with the rest of the academic staff. These notes McNab resorted into a pile of rough priority and sat them in the middle of his desk; the other piles for the rest of the staff he stacked together in one of the drawers of his desk. He picked up each statement and read it through, making a condensed summary on his computer:

> '**Dr. Edward Brown**, Director five years. Good academic reputation in research and administration; main field of study was in comparative anatomy of mammals. Went straight home to his family after five. Confirmed by wife. Stated that Dr. McKenzie had expected to take over his position when he retired but this view was not shared by the Board of Trustees. Motive:

possible friction with McKenzie on this score. Very slight motive and not possibly suggesting murder.

Dr. Sean Jamison – Head of Natural Sciences. Ten years at the museum. McKenzie's immediate superior and also seen as a candidate for the position of Director. Unmarried but states that he was at home all night. Tolerates McKenzie only because of his dedication and ability. Rivalry as a possible motive.

Dr. Fran Stewart, Head of Collections. No-nonsense type of about middle age. Seven years at the museum and solid career at various other museums in Scotland and England. Straight home to her husband and went to bed with a headache. Confirmed. Little time for McKenzie as he was seen as 'a wee nerd tae be avoided', so she had generally tried to assist with his collections as professionally as possible; not much of a motive for murder.

Dr. Harold McMahon, Head of Science and Technology. Brilliant career in industry prior to coming to the museum two years ago. Reputation for being solid and pragmatic. Went home after five and then alone to the theatre. Unconfirmed. Well-liked by all members of the staff, he had little to do with McKenzie but disliked his type of person. Motive uncertain.

Dr. Helen Gibbs, Head of Arts and Culture. Well-respected in the art world and an artist in her own right. Five years at the museum, she had a passion for nineteenth century portraits. Home with partner all night. Unconfirmed as yet. Thought McKenzie to be an 'uncouth type dealing only in bones' and so had little contact with him. Little motive.

Dr. Rory Stevens. Head of Scottish History. Speciality in the Stuart Kings. Minor clashes with McKenzie about funding but generally kept out of his way as were his collections. Lives with elderly parents but went out later for a drink. Limited motive.

Dr. Yaroslav Svoboda and **Mr. Hans Schmidt**. Visiting Fellows researching at the museum. Both started in the previous year; Schmidt doing Doctoral Studies in Recent age Megafauna and Svoboda from some obscure European university working on evolutionary trends of sauropods. Both are under the care of Director Brown. Schmidt was at his boarding house all night according to his landlady. Svoboda about middle age with an out-going in personality was enthusiastic about the museum. He had left just after five and gone to the Slovakian Club after dinner. This was confirmed by the barman who saw him at the venue that night. He had applied for a prestigious post at a southern university and had asked both Director Brown and Dr. McKenzie to be referees. Seemed to be McKenzie's only admirer and was collaborating with him on an academic paper on sauropod extinction. Both

Fellows were considered junior staff members with only limited weight in the museum hierarchy, they spent most of the time in research at the university or library. No motive for murder was apparent.

Miss Jane Tomlinson. Seconded from the University of Edinburgh doing a Masters' Degree in fluorescent minerals. Disliked McKenzie who had made some slight advances to her when she joined the staff earlier that year. She had spent most of the evening with her boyfriend at the cinema. No recent interaction with McKenzie as she had rebuffed the advances and had reported McKenzie to the Director. McKenzie subsequently avoided her. Little motive for murder.

McNab reviewed each of the notes on the academic staff again and tried to make a sociometric diagram of the relationship of each member of staff and McKenzie. There was little success in his scientific evaluation and he could only consider personal dislike or rivalry as a possible motive; neither was a convincing argument for murder.

He was looking across his desk at nothing in particular and in a state of ennui when his colleague, Detective Sergeant Olivia Kerr came up:

"Hello, Hamish. You look like 'wan o'clock half struck' as they say," she said with a smile putting a delicate hand on his shoulder.

"Oh aye! I've gone through all of these reports from the murder at the museum. I cannot find anyone who was around at the time of the murder nor had a really hard motive for doing such a callous thing." He then explained to her his brief findings at the museum and an even briefer summary of the staff. She looked at the piles of papers on the academic staff and said:

"Have you done a computer check on their backgrounds – you never know what skulduggery some of these people can get up to?"

McNab confirmed that he had already run the names of all of the staff, including the academics through the police files. Other than a few parking fines and old Willie Swayne's excellent police record, there was absolutely nothing on the museum staff.

Olivia then picked up the pile of reports on the academic staff and said, "If you wish, I'll do an internet search on social media about your boffins. There may be some common ground between McKenzie and the rest of his colleagues."

McNab looked up and grinned. "Sure. Why not! You might find that McKenzie was trolling some of the others!" he laughed. Olivia gave him a mock grimace and walked back to her desk. McNab went over his other piles of papers for the third time and then went online to find any social media sites about T-rex; any slim chance is worth it! he thought. His lack of sleep the previous night and the sheer weight of reports had put him into a depressed grey mood.

He had dropped off to sleep at his desk and had missed lunch. He woke up with a start when he heard his name being called through the thick fog within his head.

"Hamish! Wake up!"

For a moment he had a horrible thought that it was his irascible boss, Detective Chief Inspector MacFarlane. Instead, he looked up bleary-eyed into the smiling face of the lovely Detective Sergeant Olivia Kerr.

She waved a few sheets of printed paper in front of him and then brought a chair around behind his desk.

"Look here! I've found something very interesting." she said with delightful enthusiasm. "I ran all of these names through the usual social media and got back the usual trite rubbish about their personal life which was extremely boring to say the least. But!.." she emphasised the word.." when I ran the names through ProLinkNet to check on their professional activities, I got some interesting results."

McNab sat up in his chair now fully awake. "Go on!" he said.

"Well!" she continued. "All of your academic friends had accounts and posted their former alma maters and boring details of their studies. The older staff members, especially the Director and his Heads of Department also listed long and usually boring details of their many publications – what's the term? 'Publish or perish! – isn't it? The one common factor here is that most of them" – again she emphasized the word 'most' – "had books published under their own name alone or with some other co-author, usually all different. The larger collection of academic papers likewise listed papers published individually or with co-authors from a wide variety of institutions. The Director and a couple of his senior staff had been very active in the last few years and so the National Museum of Scotland appears often enough as the publisher. But…" there was that emphasis again…"your Research Fellow, Dr. Yaroslav Svoboda seems to be the odd man out."

She pulled out one sheet of paper which contained a printed list. "Look!" she said, running her finger down the list below Svoboda's name. "Absolutely all of his papers are co-authored with someone else. Moreover, when I did a cross-check on the co-authors, I found that they were relatively senior academics and the main authorities in their fields. Svoboda was the 'junior partner', as it were in each of the papers listed and the publications seemed to be from small central European universities – mostly in other languages. However, a few of the later ones are in English and from home-grown institutions, albeit rather minor ones. It looks like our Dr. Svoboda has 'stood on the shoulders of giants,' as Sir Isaac Newton once said."

McNab looked down the list of papers written by this person and Dr Svoboda, and that person with Dr. Svoboda and so on. It was far different from some of the other lists which Olivia then showed him which had a more heterogeneous list of museum staff and co-authors.

"But there's more!" Olivia said triumphantly, "Our good Doctor" she said stressing the honorific, "seems to have graduated from some vague universities not generally listed in that consulted about the top one hundred universities in Europe. I suspect that one will find that his conferring alma mater was a Degree Mill' operating out of a room somewhere in America. You get what you pay for there!"

No McNab stood up and punched the air: "Yes! Got you!" he said enthusiastically. "No clear suspect nor motive yet, but our Dr. Yaroslav Svoboda is the best candidate so far. Let's bring him in for questioning."

4.

The next day, Dr. Yaroslav Svoboda, Research Fellow at the National Museum of Scotland and a man noted for his out-going personality and good cheer was ushered into the drab interview room of Police Headquarters by a uniformed constable. The room only had a small table with two chairs placed opposite each other. They and the dull grey and dark green walls were barely illuminated by a small, barred window. There was also a shabby, uncleaned mirror on the wall near the single door. He sat there quite unsure of himself. The request by two uniformed officers that morning when he arrived at the museum, now reopened, was totally unexpected and gave him justifiable cause to worry.

McNab and Kerr watched the man through the other end of the 'shabby mirror', which was in reality a two-way mirror. There was also a small video camera and microphone in a corner of the room. These would soon be augmented by McNab's mobile phone and its voice recorder. They waited for about fifteen minutes – "Juist tae stir the pot like!" their boss, DCI MacFarlane had advised when their suspect had been put into the room. Having waited until the 'pot' had been sufficiently stirred, McNab and Kerr entered the room. McNab sat down opposite Svoboda and took his time placing his mobile phone down on the desk and activating the voice recorder app.

"I must advise you, Dr. Svoboda, that this only a preliminary interview to find out more about the murder at the museum the other day. It is being recorded and that you are at liberty to refuse to answer any questions but that anything that you say may be used in evidence against you. You have the right to have a solicitor if there is a more formal statement required but at present, we only want to find out more about the event from you." McNab said in the best severe voice that he could conjure up. Olivia stood leaning against the wall behind the suspect and had difficulty in stifling a grin. McNab pulled out an official-looking document about suspect rights and handed it to Dr. Svoboda who looked at it with some renewed confidence. He replied with a certain amount of detached arrogance: "always ready to help the members of Scotland's great constabulary," folding his hands on the table and turning around to smirk at Olivia. She looked back with a grim look of professional detachment.

When Dr. Svoboda turned back to look at McNab, he saw with some horror that the dinosaur tooth taken from the glass case in victim's office was now sitting in front of him on the table.

"Tell me, Dr. Svoboda, was it hard pulling this tooth out of McKenzie's body after you stabbed him?"

"No! It was easy, It.." he blurted out, forgetting his confidence and feeling superior to the two young detectives in the room.

"...has a grove down its length to prevent suction. Isn't that its purpose?" McNab continued his sentence.

McNab then went on to describe in detail how Svoboda had made a show of leaving the museum just after closing time and reminding the old Nightwatchman to lock up. Then he went to his club and made a point in asking the barman the time at about five thirty.

"Unfortunately," McNab said. "I later went to the club after my initial telephone call and asked other members of staff. One of the cigarette girls to whom you often paid attention, was sure that she saw you leave around six – just enough time to nip back to the museum and enter the side door using your staff key."

Svoboda slumped in his chair. It seemed that the young detective knew everything about his actions that night. McNab was slightly staggered that his suspect had given in so easy. The bravado of the man was only a thin veneer to his conniving character.

McNab then continued with the story, describing how Svoboda had surprized McKenzie who was working back as he usually did and had choked him to death. He had then turned out the light and remained quietly in the room waiting until just after the handover of the nightwatchmen at midnight. Having engaged old Willie Swayne in friendly conversation about his duties previously, he knew that Swayne always kept to a very regular routine and that he would be absent from the darkened hall for about an hour after starting his rounds. By then, the body of McKenzie was in a state of rigor mortis and could be dragged over to the T-rex skeleton, laid on his back below the jaws and then stabbed with the exhibited tooth specimen taken from the glass case. He had then returned the tooth to its original position but in his haste had forgotten to replace the small padlock. There had been a quick restoration of the room and a quick clean of the floor in case any marks due to poor McKenzie's pitiful struggles had been made on it. After the murder, he had waited until there was no sign of the nightwatchman, left by the side door and went home. McNab also stated that he had gone to Svoboda's boarding house and had found out that the landlady had complained to him the next morning about his loud and unruly return about one-thirty that night. Alibi completed.

McNab waited for some time whilst Svoboda struggled with being confronted with so many details of his night's work. Then McNab leaned over the table, gave a short nod to Olivia and said:

"Your motive, I presume had something to do with the paper which you were going to co-author with Dr. McKenzie? You seemed to have some experience in co-authoring papers with researchers who possess a greater academic standing. You were looking for yet another higher step up in your career with this paper with Dr, McKenzie, so what happened?"

Svoboda looked up, now with some tears in his eyes. He knew that his character, career and recent actions had been completely exposed. He replied slowly, in the voice of a defeated man, that McKenzie had been a very thorough man and when asked to co-author the paper had done his own research into Svoboda's academic background. McKenzie had been as astute as DS Kerr and had put several facts together and realised that his co-author had risen in the academic world by adding what little knowledge he had about each topic to the genius of his colleagues. McKenzie had realised that he was the last pawn in Svoboda's ladder climbing career. Earlier that day, McKenzie had threatened to expose the Research Assistant to the Director and the Academic world in general and had thrown him out of his office. Too engrossed in his work, McKenzie had fatally put the matter aside until the next day and so Svoboda had planned the murder. The idea about using the dinosaur tooth only had come on the spur of the moment after McKenzie had been choked. It was a bit of arrogant irony, having been continually bombarded with McKenzie's personal bragging about the T-rex and his own work which made him add the final insult. Waiting until the hall was clear, he had dragged the body under the sharp jaws of the T-rex and then inflicted the horrible wounds on the lifeless body so that all would see the fitting end to McKenzie's obsession.

McNab called in the constables outside and formally charged the disheartened man with the murder of Dr. McKenzie at the National Museum of Scotland. The case of the dragon's tooth had been solved.

About the Author

Peter Scott was born and raised in Sydney, Australia and has written over twenty-five books including non-fiction on Earth Science, the environment, survival and teaching. In the last few years, he has turned to fiction and has written in a variety of genres, mainly historical adventure, science fiction and crime. Graduating from Sydney Teachers' College he later completed part-time university studies gaining a Bachelor of Science, Masters Degrees in Science and Educational Administration and finally a Doctorate in Education. Apart from his part-time education, he has also been an Australian Army Reserve officer and Naval Cadet instructor. Having travelled extensively to all seven continents, he has always followed his own interests and so his novels often reflect his personal experiences. Scotland and Edinburgh in particular, has always been one of his favourite places and he has returned there several times. He now lives in Brisbane, Australia with his wife and extended family.

Other Fiction by the Author

Tom Shipley Series (Humour)

The Innocence of Tom Shipley: Teacher. A 19-year-old teacher reports to his first school to find that he is the Acting Head of Department. He meets many interesting characters in his first years of teaching.

Tom Shipley's War, Memoirs of a Weekend Warrior. 1965 and the first ballot for Australian conscripts for the Vietnam War. With many of his friends drafted and the protest movement now directed against them, Tom Shipley enlists into the local Army Reserve unit and finds a new enemy; the Army itself.

Tall Ships Series (Historical Science Fiction)

The Ice Ship. 1840 and an advanced steam-auxiliary whaling ship sets out from New England to go whaling in Antarctic waters. A freak storm of cold weather sends it further south and it becomes embedded in the ice. Panicked, the crew desert and leave their young captain on board. This is a tale about their survival.

Two Hundred Years before the Mast, An Adventure in Time. It is 1996 and a young Nuclear Physicist accidently discovers how to travel in time. Having an interest in the days of fighting sail, he goes back to the year 1796 where he is unexpectedly press ganged aboard a Royal Navy frigate. How does he survive the peril in which his ship is placed?

<u>San Rafael Series</u> (Historical Adventure -written as 'Hernan Moreno Ruiz')

Letters from San Rafael. It is 1880 and Peruvian intelligence officer, Colonel Moreno and his Sergeant, Garcia, are captured by the Ecuadorians during a border dispute and taken to the supply depot of San Rafael in Ecuador. Treated as guests by the old Comandante, Moreno is able to smuggle letters home. They each tell a separate tale about South America and its people at that time as told to Morano by the people of San Rafael.

Return to San Rafael. Ten years on and Moreno and Garcia are called upon by their former captors to return to the now deserted hacienda of San Rafael to discover its secret which will affect the future of both Peru and Ecuador. Along the way they hear many stories of the places through which they travel and meet the mysterious Father Xavier, a Jesuit priest who knows more about their secret mission than they do.

Confessions of Father Xavier. Set in the 1870's, this is the story of how a young Peruvian cavalry officer becomes the mysterious Jesuit priest, Father Xavier and the many adventures he has before becoming an agent for both the Church and Government.

Australian Bush Stories (Short Stories)

Cry of the Currawong. A series of short, connected and humorous stories about Australian country life in the 1950's and how a young boy from the city finds many adventures with his new-found cousins, uncles and aunts.

Orion and Other Stories of the Future

This is a trilogy of science fiction stories set in the near future:

Orion – with air transport uncertain and limited to small aircraft, the *Orion*, is a new innovation based on a past concept. However, its first flight is jeopardised by the treat of sabotage. Only Head of Security, Troy Jaeger knows for certain who is trying to destroy Project Orion. Can the saboteur be stopped before the *Orion* is destroyed?

Download – in the future, education has become fully computerised and students receive direct downloads of the knowledge, skills and attitudes required directly into their brainstem. A perfect system where nothing can go wrong. Or can it?

Steelwind – four yachtsmen find the giant, five masted cargo sailing ship apparently deserted in the vast Southern Ocean. Boarding her, they find the bodies of the Captain and First Officer dead on the Bridge. An attempt is also made on their lives and they sense that they are not alone on the huge windjammer.

Non-Fiction

The author has also written over twenty reference books on Earth Science, Environmental Science, Global Warming, Teaching and Survival in the Field. All are available as Kindle eBooks (view on any device with the free Kindle App) and in print form (available from the publisher at info.felixpublishing@gmail.com

www.ingramcontent.com/pod-product-compliance
Lightning Source LLC
Chambersburg PA
CBHW070949180726
48291CB00004B/1209